Tainted

Jamie Begley

Tainted

ISBN-13: 978-0615973159
ISBN-10: 0615973159

Prologue

The sound of the door opening barely registered in her cloudy mind. She was no longer able to wonder about or be afraid of who was entering the room. Sawyer felt completely detached from her body. A body that was unable to respond to her commands.

The stray strand of hair that had fallen across her eyes had become an irritant, but she had been unable to raise her hand to brush it away.

Someone would come every so often and carry her limp body to the bathroom and order her to use the toilet. She had been shamed to the core of her soul to have to use it in front of the man watching from the doorway. He hadn't even bothered to shut the door, leaving it open so that anyone passing by could see within the room.

Her full bladder had her wishing someone would come soon; even the humiliating experience was better than suffering with the basic desire to relieve herself. So far, she had managed not to wet herself, but she didn't know how much longer before that humiliation would happen.

The light coming on in the room had her jerking involuntary; the pain in her eyes from the light was like shards of glass. A low whimper escaped her dry mouth.

"Shut the fuck up," the hateful voice said from the foot of the cot she was handcuffed to.

Sawyer felt movement next to her as the man brushed against her cot before he leaned over the cot next to hers. She hadn't been able to make out the woman handcuffed to the cot next to her, or the other women in the room. All she heard was their crying in the dark. Several of them called out in their terror for their family. Sawyer knew because she had awoken several times herself, crying a name. It was the same name every time she had awoken to the discovery she had been kidnapped.

Vida.

She was the only family she had left, and they weren't even related by blood. They were friends who had grown up together, becoming as close as sisters. They even shared a rundown apartment in the same neighborhood that they had grown up in, in Queen City, Texas.

Sawyer finally managed to turn her head, seeing the man who had taken her to the bathroom, going from cot to cot, turning the women so he could look at them.

"Dammit to hell! Get your ass in here!"

"What are you yelling for?"

"You left marks on every fucking one of them! I told you not to leave marks! What in the fuck am I supposed to do now?"

"What does it matter?" The sullen voice roused Sawyer from falling back asleep, but the pain in her bladder needed to be relieved.

"Redman's a woman short. One got sick, vomiting everywhere. We can't have them puking while someone's trying to fuck them."

"What are we supposed to do?"

"We were supposed to send one of these cunts, but you've got them so bruised up we can't send any of them. Briggs is going to kick your ass."

"He doesn't have to know. There has to be one in here

that's not marked."

"I've looked at every fucking one of them asswipe. What are you going to do?"

"Me?" Tommy's voice had an edge of fear. Sawyer felt a spurt of satisfaction.

"Yeah, you."

Sawyer drifted away again, but the cramp in her belly woke her back up.

"Please, I need to use the restroom," she moaned.

"I told you to shut up!"

"I have to go." Sawyer began crying. If they didn't take her, she wouldn't be able to hold it much longer, and she couldn't bear the humiliation of peeing on herself.

"Dammit."

Sawyer felt the metal cuff around her wrist open, and then her wrist fell numbly by her side. A rough hand jerked her up, half-carrying and half-dragging her across the tiled floor. Pushing her into the bathroom, he stood in the doorway, watching as she fumbled with the sweatpants she had woken up wearing.

"She doesn't have a mark on her," Tommy said.

"We can't send her. Briggs said Digger has plans for her."

"How long does Redman need the woman for his client?"

"Just for tonight."

"Digger doesn't even have to know."

"She's not even trained yet."

"We'll give her another dose. It'll keep her quiet. She doesn't have to be trained to fuck; she just has to keep her legs open." Both men laughed as she finished, almost falling over while pulling up her sweatpants.

"Get her dressed then. I'll call Redman and tell him she'll be ready in thirty."

Chapter One

"How's everything going on the road?" Grace asked.

"Couldn't be better," Kaden answered, absently stroking the back of one of the women in bed with him. After the concert, he had picked two from the mass of followers, who trailed after them from concert to concert, hoping for the chance to come into contact with the band members.

Silence met his response. Kaden rolled to his back as the other fan crawled between his legs, stroking his dick. His hand went to her hair as his hips lifted, putting his cock into her experienced mouth.

"Kaden, I'm staying with Mom while James looks for a job in Nashville. Why don't you sneak away for a few days between concerts? It's been awhile since you've seen Abby and Adam; they're getting older. I want them to get to know you better. You haven't seen them for six months. Mom misses you…" As usual, when his sister talked, she didn't pause for breath.

"Can't right now. Too busy. Maybe in a few months. I have a week off for Thanksgiving; me and Tatiana will come for a visit." Kaden let his hands go to the other woman's breast as the other one sucked his dick.

"Oh, okay."

He ignored the disappointment in her voice.

"I have to go, Grace, someone's calling my name. Tell Mom I said, hi." Kaden hung up the phone before his sister was even able to say goodbye.

The axe swung down, breaking the log cleanly as the two pieces fell to the side of the stump. Kaden bent down, picking up another log and placing it on the stump. Lifting the axe, he swung down, using all his strength. Again, the log split into pieces. Over and over, Kaden repeated the process until there were only a few pieces left to split. As he chopped, he heard the steps approach from behind him and then paused as a familiar, sardonic voice rang out in the silence of the yard. "I think you have enough wood, Kaden."

Kaden stiffened, but didn't stop chopping the wood until he had finished the remaining logs. Breathing heavily, sweat dripped off him and soaked the thin t-shirt he was wearing.

"What do you want, R.J.?"

R.J. moved to pick up a few of the logs that Kaden had split, carrying them to the woodpile against the cabin.

"We need to talk," R.J. said, bending down to pick up more wood.

"You're going to ruin that expensive suit."

R.J. shrugged as he stacked the wood neatly. Together they worked in silence, stacking the wood. When they finished, Kaden went inside the cabin without a word. R.J. followed behind, taking a seat at the table after washing his hands at the sink.

Kaden ignored him as he picked up the coffee cup he had left sitting on the counter. He took another from the cabinet, pouring both cups to the brim with coffee and then carried them to the table. He sat one down in front of R.J. before taking a seat for himself.

"What do you want, R.J.?"

"Jesse's been hurt in a car accident." R.J. winced at the first taste of the strong coffee.

"How bad?"

"Two broken ribs, fractured arm and a broken leg."

"That sucks for you, doesn't it, with the new tour starting?"

"How did you know about the tour starting?"

"Ax," Kaden answered, finishing his coffee and then getting up to put his cup in the sink.

"I can't say I'm surprised he's the only one you kept in contact with, but it would've been nice him telling me a week ago, instead of letting me go to three different states looking for you." R.J. didn't try to hide his frustration.

"That's why I kept in touch with him; he was the only one in the band who knew how to keep his mouth shut." Kaden's harsh voice had R.J. wincing as his words rang home.

When R.J. would have spoken again, Kaden cut him off. "Get to the point. What do you want, R.J.?"

"I need you to take over for Jesse. You're the only one who could bring in the revenue that Jesse would have."

Kaden couldn't help himself from laughing in his former tour manager's face.

"Prop Jesse up on a stool if you have to, but there is no way in hell I'm stepping back on a stage."

"Jesse already spent his advance on concert sales, so unless he can pay back the advance, he's going to lose his home. Ax isn't in much better shape; his child support payments have been taking a large chunk of his money. If he has to pay back the advance, then that new recording studio he's so proud of, is going to close before a record could even be produced. D-mon can't —"

"Stop, R.J. I can see where this is headed. You should know by now that I haven't got a sympathetic bone left in my body. If that's the best you've got, I have things to do."

"I didn't want to do this, Kaden, but I will if I have to. I won't let the band suffer because you've buried yourself in grief."

"Shut up, R.J., and get out. We're done talking."

"I'll send the press the tapes," R.J. threatened.

Kaden lost it. Taking a step forward, he jerked R.J. to his feet and then slung him toward the door.

R.J. managed to right himself before turning back to face an intimidating, furious Kaden. "I mean it, Kaden. Do the tour and they're yours. I'll hand them over and you'll never see me again," R.J. promised.

Kaden picked up R.J.'s empty cup and threw it against the kitchen wall. Taking a deep breath, he then released it, while getting himself back under control, before he killed R.J. with his bare hands.

"I have no choice it seems, R.J.; if you don't give me the tapes, I'll—"

"You do the concert, and they're yours." R.J. didn't look away.

Kaden had no choice other than to believe him.

"When's the first concert?" Kaden wanted those tapes back. If he had to tour the next year to get them back, then he would do it. Raking his hand through his long hair, he waited for R.J. to answer his question.

"In three weeks. I booked them pretty heavily."

"You always did," Kaden said sarcastically. "Get out, R.J.; you've accomplished what you wanted."

"Kaden, if I had a choice, I would have left you alone. I let you leave without trying to stop you, didn't I? I can't let everyone down; there are too many people who are depending on me. I'm sorry." R.J. went to the door and opened it. Kaden watched his former manager go out the door, closing it behind him.

He had sworn when he had walked away that he would never sing again. For five years, he had kept that promise, and now he was going to have to return. Kaden already knew what was ahead of him; months of no sleep, no personal space and miles and miles of road. Once, a tour of this magnitude would have been worth celebrating; now, it was only a reminder of how fucked up he had been.

Cleaning up the mess he had made, Kaden went into the back bedroom, which was empty except for the bed and dresser. Going to the closet, he packed his bag with what few items he possessed. He then sat down on the bed, staring at the picture he had taped to the wall by his bed. Reaching out, he carefully removed the worn picture, and then held it in his hand as he stared at it for several moments, before placing it in his bag. Afterward, he got up, took a quick shower, and then went to bed. Lying naked on the bed, he listened to the quiet night, feeling his body finally relax for the first time since R.J. had left.

Tomorrow, he would close the cabin then catch a plane to Dallas. For five years, he had dodged the fame of his career; now, he was going to have to face the publicity of his return and the circumstances that had caused his departure. They would all be waiting and watching for him to resume his wild lifestyle.

The women, drugs and money had all been the rewards of the career that he had used and exploited. This time around, none of it held any appeal. Instead, he would save Mouth2Mouth from financial disaster and get the tapes that had been held over his head for five years. The man who had left was not the one returning this time; this man had nothing left to lose.

Chapter Two

"Did you get the pictures I sent?" Grace asked.

"Not yet, my mail hasn't caught up with me," Kaden answered as he made four small lines of coke with his platinum card.

"Oh." Disappointment filled his sister's voice. "That's okay; I have more of them trick or treating. They looked so cute. I dressed them up as—"

Kaden laid the phone down, doing two lines before picking his cell phone back up.

"—Adam made himself sick eating too much candy, of course."

Kaden could tell this was going to go on for a while. "Grace, R.J. is calling on another line, I have to go. Tell Mom, I said hi."

"But don't you want to talk to her?"

"Next time; I have to go." Kaden disconnected the call, already bending over to do the remaining two lines of white powder.

Kaden's fingers moved over the guitar as the conversation played in his mind, bringing the end to the concert that had filled the arena to capacity. With a wave, he exited the stage as each of the band members followed his cue.

"Kaden, that was great! I thought you would have

trouble learning all the new material, but you didn't miss a fucking note." D-mon slapped him on the back as they waited in the VIP room for their car to be brought to the back exit. They had a two-day layover in San Antonio before they would leave for their next gig, so they were staying at a hotel tonight.

R.J. stuck his head in the door. "The car is here."

Four security guards were waiting outside the door as they exited the arena. The huge crowd waiting outside screamed their names when they saw the band.

"Kaden!" a young blonde girl that barely looked legal, pulled her top down, exposing her breasts. He kept on walking.

Ax tried to make his way to the woman, but R.J. held him back. "I already have entertainment for you back at the hotel. Get in the car, Ax."

"You're taking all the fun out of getting laid." Kaden heard Ax complain as he slid into the car next to him.

"I'm trying to save you another DNA test for child support," R.J. snapped, closing the door.

Kaden ignored the conversation as the car pulled out into the heavy traffic, leaving the arena. The drive back to the hotel took fifteen minutes in the car with the others hyped up from the show.

"It's good to have you back."

Kaden looked across the seat at Sin. "You're still the master with the drums, Sin."

Sin stared back at him with a reserved smile. He could be the most laid back of the band members or the wildest, depending on the mood he was in and what he was doing. Alcohol made him everyone's best buddy; drugs made him a mean son of a bitch, wanting to fight everyone he came into contact with. Kaden thought both sides of him were an asshole, and he had the least to do with him, compared to the other band members.

The car drove to the back entrance of the hotel, coming to a stop.

"Thanks, Alec." Kaden stepped out of the limo when Alec—the head of security who Kaden had hired, rejecting the firm that R.J. usually went with—opened the door. It had caused an argument between them, but R.J. had conceded when he saw that Kaden wasn't going to back down.

"It's clear. The press thinks you're across at the Prestige. It'll take them a couple of hours to figure out where you're at," Alec told him, closing the car door after the others had exited.

Kaden and the rest of the group followed Alec through the empty kitchen and into the private elevator that the staff used. The elevator stopped at the top floor and everyone got off, going to the lone door.

Alec caught Kaden's arm before he could move forward. "R.J. had several women escorted here before the show started. Rick Redman brought them then took off. Said he would be back in the morning."

Kaden's lips tightened. He had met Rick several years ago when he had first started out. He was known for providing call girls for those well known in the entertainment industry. He had acquaintances who had used his service repeatedly, saving themselves the hassle of the tabloid exposé's, or—like Ax—the numerous paternity claims from their one-night stands.

He had never been tempted by any of Rick's girls, preferring to pick women from the followers that trailed after the band.

"When did R.J. become involved with Redman?"

"This is the first tour that R.J. has used his services." Alec's disgusted voice left no doubt of his opinion of Redman. "He paid thirty-thousand out six months ago to keep Jesse's wife from finding out about a weekend in the Caribbean with a nineteen-year-old."

"I'm surprised R.J. paid to keep it quiet; he used to love the publicity." Kaden was already able to hear the noise of the party from the outside of the hotel room. "I don't care how many whores he hires, as long as they stay away from me," Kaden said, going in the hotel room.

The sight that met his eyes was one he had seen many times. At least five women were seated around the room with Sin and D-mon already pouring out drinks. Ax was already talking to a pretty brunette.

His condition of no drugs had aroused arguments from the three group members, but his threat to walk had been taken seriously. Kaden didn't doubt his ability to withstand the temptation of the drugs he had once enjoyed; he just didn't want another reminder of how fucked up he had been.

"Which room is mine?" Kaden asked R.J., who had a woman already sitting on his lap.

He pointed toward the hallway to the left. "I had your bag put in the last one down the hall so you wouldn't be disturbed by the noise."

A delicate arm slid around his neck as a lush blonde leaned against him, plastering her tits against his chest.

"I can keep you company, Daddy." One of her arms glided from his neck downwards, grasping his hip as she pushed her pussy against his dick. Kaden's dick didn't move behind his zipper. Her dark blue eyes were glazed and her thickened voice was incentive enough to take both of her hands into his, moving away from her touch.

"No, thanks; I'll pass." Even when he had reached the pinnacle of his career, he hadn't paid for pussy.

Kaden walked down the hallway of the suite, ignoring Ax and D-mon's yells to return. Opening the closed door, he went into the darkened room without bothering to turn on the light since the bathroom light had been left on, illuminating half of the room. He went into the bathroom, shutting the door behind him. Getting undressed, he turned the shower on then stepped inside, letting the hot water relax his tired muscles. He let the warm spray run over his body before grabbing the soap and washing the sweat from the hot lights of the concert away, as well as the smell of the whore's musky perfume.

Stepping out of the shower, he dried off before using the blow dryer to dry his hair. His shorter hair, which he had cut yesterday to avoid any resemblance to the wild rocker he had been five years ago, dried quickly. When it was dry enough not to wet the sheets, he left the bathroom, leaving the door ajar enough to see the path to the bed where the covers had already been turned down for the night. He wasn't a kid anymore; he didn't feel the adrenaline rush that came after each show. Tonight, he was tired and ready for sleep after the hectic day leading up to the concert. The concert had taken the last of his reserves. He was going to have to build himself back up to performing the long hours again.

"What the fuck?" Kaden's feet tripped over something lying on the floor. Unable to prevent his fall, he fell across the object, half on and half off the person lying unconscious on the floor. He knew they were unconscious because they didn't move or make a sound when he put out a hand out to find what he had fallen over. The only reason he knew they were still alive was because of the warmth of the skin he touched.

Clumsily managing to get to his feet, he bent down to lift the person onto the bed before turning on the bedside lamp. The bright light had him blinking several seconds until he could focus on the woman lying on his bed.

Muttering angrily to himself, he reached out to shake the woman's shoulder to wake her, stopping when she opened her eyes. Kaden stared down into eyes the color of golden honey. Her face was exquisite; all fine angles and high cheekbones with a mouth meant to please. Her flame-red hair highlighted in the lamplight with a golden glow.

Kaden had dated and fucked several models during his career, the first one when he was fourteen, and while this woman wasn't as beautiful, she had a fragile appearance as if she was one of the dolls that had sat on his niece's shelf because she had been too afraid to play with it, afraid it would break.

Five years ago, he would have climbed into bed with this woman and spent the night banging her, but those nights were long gone.

"Get your ass up and get out."

Chapter Three

Sawyer blinked her eyes as she tried to clear her blurry vision. She had heard the man staring down at her, but she couldn't make her fuzzy mind understand his words.

She opened her lips to try to ask for help, but the noise that escaped her dry mouth was a whimper.

The man's eyes narrowed on her and his expression turned to one of disgust. Sawyer trembled in the cold room; she wanted to borough under the blankets for warmth, yet she couldn't make her arms and legs move. She could only lie there helplessly, waiting to see what the stranger would do next.

He bent down, jerking her into a sitting position. When she started to slide back down onto the bed, he placed a hand on her shoulder, holding her still.

"Rick has really outdone himself this time. Overdid it, didn't you?"

She saw him take a cell phone out of his pocket and punch in numbers. She tried to listen to the conversation, but the fog that was attacking her brain made her just want to close her eyes and go to sleep.

"Stay awake, dammit." He roughly shook her shoulder,

startling her into opening her eyes. "That's it. I've sent for someone to take you home."

Relief inundated her body at his words and tears flooded her eyes as she thought of Vida's reaction when she walked through the door of the apartment they shared. Vida would take care of her; she would get her the help that she needed.

The stranger lifted her limp body to lean back against the headboard. She tried to turn her head to see where he went, but her head fell limply to the side.

She heard the water running nearby then a hand was lifting her head back upright. "What in the hell did you take?" his harsh voice asked.

Sawyer was unable to answer him as a glass was placed against her lips. She greedily drank the cold water, feeling the soothing relief as it went down her burning throat. She didn't remember the last time they had given her more to drink than a sip of water.

"Slow down; you're going to make yourself sick." Sawyer tried to slow down, but she was afraid he would take it away before she was finished; however, he took it away when she didn't slow down anyway. She heard him set it on the nightstand.

She was about to beg for it back when she heard a knock on the door. He rose from sitting on the side of the bed, opening it to a man dressed in dark jeans and a black leather jacket.

"What's going on, Kaden?" the man questioned.

"Alec, she's messed up pretty bad. I found her when I came in here to go to bed."

The blond man moved to the side of the bed. She tried to look up at him, but fell sideways, her head almost banging against the nightstand. The man who had given her the water managed to catch her just before impact, lifting her back against the bed.

"I thought she looked out of it when Redman dropped her off, but two other women were beside her, talking to her. Kaden, I'm sorry. I should have followed my instincts and told them to go, but Redman was adamant that R.J. wanted them here when the band finished the concert."

"It's not your fault, Alec. It's R.J.'s. Redman is trouble, but he gives his clients pussy without the hassle." His disgusted voice disturbed Sawyer as she tried to understand what the two men were talking about.

"What do you want me to do with her?" The one named Alec looked at the man who had said he was going to take her home. "Want me to take her into the other room?"

Sawyer managed to shake her head, groaning when the movement sent shards of pain through her skull.

"No, they're so out of it by now; they won't even notice she's fucked up," he sighed, running his hand through his dark hair.

Sawyer looked up at him, attempting without words to plead for help. She tried to get her thickened tongue to move to tell him to call the police.

"Take her home."

Sawyer couldn't prevent the tears slipping down her cheeks at his words.

Bending down he spoke to her. "Where do you live?"

Again she tried to speak, but couldn't, crying harder.

Sighing, he rose to stand up, towering over her. "Go outside, Alec, and ask the other girls where she lives."

Frantically, she shook her head, fear giving her strength as she tried to rise from the bed. Instead, she flopped down, wiggling on the mattress like a fish dragged out of the water.

"Okay, calm down. We get the message." The one named Kaden straightened her legs until she lay down straight on the mattress. "What now?" he asked the man named Alec.

"The only thing we can do. We wait until she can tell us where to take her or give her back to Redman when he shows up later to pick them up."

Sawyer managed with the last of her strength to grab the one named Kaden's hand when he sat down on the side of the bed beside her. Her nails dug into his flesh. Both men stared down at her with frowns at her frightened reaction.

"Well, she answered that question," Alec said, moving beside Kaden to touch her wrist with a light touch, searching for her pulse. She felt him press down on her wrist when he found it.

"Her pulse is slow but steady. She should be more coherent by morning. If not, we can take her to the hospital."

"She likes that idea," Kaden said when she managed to nod.

"I don't like this, Kaden. She seems scared of Redman."

Kaden frowned as her golden eyes searched his, trying without words to ask for the help she needed. "I don't understand. The other women seemed a little high, but not scared. Redman has been doing this for years. If there was something shady going on, surely someone would have put the word out by now."

"Not if they didn't want the publicity," Alec corrected him.

Kaden lifted the water glass, while Alec helped her sit up again. This time she drank the water more slowly. She had almost finished the glass when he took it away.

"I'll go out into the other room and ask the girls a few questions; see what I can find out. I'll get something for her to eat also. It'll help get the drugs out of her system. Get her some more water; keep her hydrated."

"All right." Sawyer watched as the blond man disappeared back through the bedroom door.

Kaden left her side, going back into the bathroom and running more water into the now empty glass. Sawyer waited for the glass of water, and when she felt the glass pressed against her lips, she drank as much as she could before nudging the glass away with her chin.

"Had enough?" This time Sawyer managed to nod her head. Drowsiness was coming over her full force. She tried to fight it, afraid if she went back to sleep, she would find herself back in that dark room, handcuffed to the cot again.

As if reading her mind, she felt the mattress sink down next to her. "Go to sleep. It'll help get the drugs out of your system. Nothing will happen until you wake."

Doubtfully, she stared up at him, feeling her lips tremble. It was only when she heard his soft whisper that she allowed her eyes to close, letting the fog carry her away.

"I promise."

* * *

Kaden stared down at the young woman lying on his hotel bed. His instincts were screaming at him that something was going on here, and it was more than just a prostitute hired to entertain for a few hours.

His worry was confirmed when Alec slipped back into the bedroom, coming to stand next to him.

"When I tried to get any information off them, they just shook their heads and changed the subject. They looked as scared as her," Alec nodded his head toward the woman lying unconscious, "when I mentioned Rick."

"Fuck."

They stared at each other, trying to figure out their next move.

"If we call the cops then Mouth2Mouth will be all over the news by morning. Redman is supposed to be back in the morning to bring the car and pick the girls up, but we can offer them an escort home if they don't want to go with him. When she wakes up, she should be able to tell us where to take her. The best case scenario here is that they'll all keep their mouths closed."

"I hope this works. Redman is going to be furious when he shows up in the morning, Kaden."

"Order extra security. I don't know where he gets these women, but I want to be prepared for anything."

Alec moved away from the bed, pulling out his cell phone.

Kaden didn't wake the woman to get her to eat the food Alec had brought back, hoping the sleep would clear her mind so they would know where to take her. He wanted her out of his hair before the press got hold of this story. He could practically see the headlines. They wouldn't care that she was already drugged before coming to the hotel room. It would be disastrous enough that the group had bought prostitutes for the night.

It was going to be dicey, dealing with Redman, but he couldn't hand over the women in good conscience, knowing something was wrong with the set up. He was going to do what he could for the women while still protecting Mouth2Mouth.

Chapter Four

Sawyer woke carefully, turning her head slowly on the pillow. The cloudiness that had affected her brain was gone, but her thought process still felt slow. She looked around the same hotel room she had found herself in last night. Sunlight was trying to filter through the dark curtains.

"She's awake." Her head turned toward the men, who she felt move to the side of the bed. She hadn't been able to see them clearly last night, though she could remember the dark haired one had been called Kaden and the blond one Alec.

"W—where am I?" Her dry throat barely let the words pass through her cracked lips.

"You're in my hotel room. Rick Redman brought you and several other women to our suite last night. Do you remember?" The one named Kaden spoke first.

Sawyer nodded her head, putting a hand to her head when it set off a pounding pain in her temple. She licked her lips, trying to get the pain back under control. "I—I— need to get out of here before he gets back." She tried to rise up, but her pounding temple was the least of her problems when her stomach began heaving.

"She's going to vomit." Kaden's voice was grim as he lifted her and carried her to the bathroom.

Setting her bare feet on the cool floor, she fell to her knees beside the toilet that thankfully seemed clean, before emptying her already empty stomach. Dry heaves racked her body as both men silently watched. When she finally finished, Kaden handed her a glass of cool liquid, which tasted like ginger ale and calmed her churning stomach. A wet cloth was then put in her hand to wash her face. She sucked in a calming breath as she handed the cloth back.

Sawyer tried to get to her feet and found a hand gently lifting her as she caught a glance at herself in the mirror. Her naturally pale skin was parchment white, and her eyes were huge, staring back in fright, when she saw both men were watching her reaction. Turning back to the men, she knew she needed their help. She could only pray they would listen.

"I—I n—n—need to get out of here before Rick comes back for us," she repeated her earlier request, trying to get the words passed her lips, though she was too upset to be frustrated by her usual stutter.

"Don't worry about Redman," Kaden said.

Sawyer threw him a disbelieving look. The stranger didn't have a clue who he was dealing with.

"The rest of the women are in the other room, and we're going to see they get home safely."

Sawyer trembled as she stared at the two men. The taller one was lean with hair that was short but full. He was wearing jeans and a thin t-shirt. His looks were such that they would make any woman pause and take a second glance. He had an air of sensuality that she had only seen a few times in her life.

The blond, while not as tall, was more muscular with unruly hair. He was wearing dark jeans with a dark t-shirt and a leather jacket. Neither of these men were aware of the quicksand they were stepping into, and she couldn't stop them if she wanted to save herself.

A cold chill struck her, raising goose bumps on her barely-covered flesh. Gazing down at herself, she saw that she was wearing a revealing black dress that came to the tops of her thighs with tiny straps and a revealing slit between her breasts. A thin, golden chain barely held the material together.

"Let me see if I can find you something warmer." Kaden went in search for something, while Alec helped her out of the bathroom to sit in a chair in the bedroom. Sawyer gratefully sank down on the elegant chair, while she watched Kaden pull a zippered hoodie from a large, black bag.

"I'm afraid this is all I have," he apologized.

Sawyer took it from his hand, putting the warm material on her chilled body. His scent clung to the fleece material, somehow reassuring her that she was finally out of her nightmare.

"Y—you have to call the police," Sawyer urged. "Now. Before Rick gets back."

Both men stared at her in surprise before both of their expressions turned grim.

"What's going on?" Alec asked, bending down before her.

Sawyer ran a hand through her tangled hair, wincing as she unintentionally pulled at the tangled mess. "He kidnapped me." She saw both men staring at each other.

"We'll call the police of course, but do you know how you ended up here?" Alec asked, sympathy in his eyes.

Sawyer nodded, finally becoming warm. "They sent me here because the other women were too badly hurt." She paused before continuing, "I've never seen the women who are in the other room before, but I'm sure they're like the others and have no choice. They drugged me before Rick showed up to bring me here."

Sawyer's fuzzy mind finally began to connect the dots; her eyes darkened in fear as she carefully studied the two men. She leaped off the chair, knocking Alec down, trying to reach the door, however, an arm around her waist caught her, bringing her back against his hard body. Her back pressed against his chest as she struggled against his firm hold.

"Settle down. We're not going to hurt you. We're trying to help you," Kaden said, placing her back in the chair.

"Then call the police!" Sawyer yelled at them.

"All right." Alec pulled out his phone, preparing to make the call, when the bedroom door slammed open and a man with wild eyes came rushing into the room.

"There she is. She needs to go. Redman started freaking out when he didn't see her. He's here to pick her and the other women up. He's pulled a gun on Ax." Alec ran from the room, leaving the others behind.

"Lock the door," Kaden ordered as he followed closely behind Alec.

Sawyer jumped up, frantically looking for a phone. Seeing one on the nightstand by the bed, she ran to it and lifted the receiver. The man who had come in warning Kaden and Alec, jerked it away, ripping the cord out of the wall.

"You're not calling the press. The whole reason I hired you sluts was so that they wouldn't become involved."

"Are you crazy?" Sawyer screamed at him. "I was calling the police." She saw the man pale as he pushed her toward the doorway.

"You're not calling anyone until I find out what's going on here. If anyone is going to call the cops, it's going to be me." He dragged her struggling body down the hallway toward the large room everyone was gathered in, facing Redman. He came to an abrupt stop when he saw what was going on in the tension-filled room.

Sawyer didn't have to tell the man he had fucked up. It was obvious when they entered to find Rick standing with a gun to a man's head and two other men standing in the doorway with guns pointed at the group of people standing there.

"It's about fucking time, Sawyer. We were waiting on you." Rick gave her his smarmy smile, which made Sawyer's weak stomach want to throw up the small amount of ginger ale she had drunk. "Let's go." He motioned for the women, who all moved toward Rick.

"These women aren't going anywhere with you, Redman. I've already told you that."

"You don't have a choice, Kaden. These are my bitches to do with as I want. Now move before I lose what patience I have left, and you have to audition for a new guitarist."

Sawyer weakly braced her hand on the wall beside her, afraid she was going to pass out.

"Put the guns away. You're not going to shoot. We both know that there are cameras all over the hotel." Kaden kept talking to Rick as if he wasn't frightened for his friend, while Sawyer just wanted to run screaming from the evil man.

"I'll be long gone, and you and all your buddies will be dead." Rick shrugged. "It's not the first time I'll have to disappear, and it sure as shit won't be the last." Rick gave a grin that had her blood turning cold. He was telling them this wouldn't be the first time he had killed, and his casual shrug left no doubt he was telling the truth.

"There is no need to go to these extremes. We can come to an agreement that will make us both happy," Kaden countered, immediately getting Rick's attention.

"Like what?"

"You want to make money off these women? Then sell them to me," Kaden said.

Sawyer couldn't believe the words coming out of his mouth. Was he just trying to pacify Rick so that the guns would be put away or was he serious?

Rick's greedy eyes went over the five women trembling in terror and withdrawal from the drugs that had been pumped into them. "Four hundred thousand."

"Deal. We'll transfer the money into your account first thing in the morning." Kaden didn't haggle over the price of the abused women.

"I'm afraid I can't take your word for it, Kaden." Turning, Rick shoved the man he was holding at gunpoint to the two men standing in the doorway. They took him, disappearing. Kaden took a step toward the now empty doorway.

"Back off. He'll be fine for a day until I get my money in the morning. I'll even feed him breakfast before I bring him back." Rick's mocking voice had Sawyer cringing.

What had she ever seen in the man—other than his good looks—that had drawn her attention while she was waitressing in an upscale restaurant? He had charmed her into giving him her address and going out on a date after just a few meetings. She felt as if he had somehow tainted her by even having been briefly acquainted with him.

"I don't suppose I have to tell you that our transaction should remain private? Any of these bitches open their mouths to the cops, my boss won't be happy."

"I'll make sure no one opens their mouth," Kaden replied to his threat.

"You do that. That money you'll be placing in my account will make sure I have enough to disappear on. My boss won't be happy to move his operation, but you'll be the one left to deal with him." Rick pointed the gun toward Sawyer. "Let's go."

Sawyer's full bladder almost emptied on her as the gun turned toward her.

Kaden moved to stand in front of the gun pointed at her. "She's not going anywhere. She's part of the deal." Kaden's angry voice gave Sawyer hope.

"No. My life wouldn't be worth shit if I come back without her. The boss has plans for her."

"What plans?" Kaden didn't move, blocking Sawyer from Rick's sight.

"How the fuck do I know? He doesn't exactly tell me

his business. Move it, Sawyer."

"If she's not for sale, how about a rental?" Kaden bargained.

Rick's avarice made him pause.

"How about one hundred thousand a month until I return her?" Sawyer couldn't believe the sum of money Kaden was discussing as if it was nothing. Even the man that had dragged her from the bedroom tried to interrupt.

"Kaden—"

"Shut up, R.J.," he snapped, and surprisingly the man didn't argue.

"Now that might be a deal my boss could live with." Taking a cell phone out of his pocket, he dialed a number while keeping the gun trained on the occupants of the room.

Sawyer looked around the expensive hotel room, seeing two other men who were sitting tensely on the couch. Both seemed more angry than scared. Sawyer could only shake her head at their stupidity. They still didn't grasp who they were dealing with, thinking that their money was going to buy them out of this situation. It would, but only temporarily. Besides, it remained to be seen if it was even going to save her butt.

Her attention was brought back to Rick when he disconnected the call. "It's your lucky day, Kaden. My boss is in a good mood with the money I made him today." The gun was now pointed in Sawyer's direction. "He said to give you a message, Sawyer." Taking a step to the side, Rick made sure she had a clear view of him and the gun. "He said that if you had any thought about running or calling the police that Vida would be your replacement."

Fear struck her heart. "Don't you dare touch Vida." Sawyer moved toward him, but Kaden caught her by the waist, pulling her against his side.

"Then keep your fucking mouth closed. I will personally break in that sweet thing if you don't." The gleam in his eyes said he was already thinking about the damage he would inflict on her friend.

Sawyer began crying; she couldn't hold it back any longer. The fear that her friend, who was more like a sister, could be hurt because of her mistake was more than she could handle.

"As for you, bitches, I know you will keep your mouths closed because you know what will happen if he becomes angry." The frightened women all shook their heads. *They were just as frightened as she was*, Sawyer thought. Plus they had been on the drugs longer, and now it would be leaving their bodies in a state of painful withdrawals.

"Good, I'm glad we understand each other." Turning toward the door, he gave his parting threat. "I'll be waiting on my money, Kaden." He was gone several seconds before Alec rushed out the door, his cell phone in his hand.

"It's all right; he's gone." Kaden's reassuring voice had Sawyer trying to stop her hysterical tears. When she didn't stop, Kaden lifted her up and carried her back into the bathroom, located in the bedroom they had come from.

Turning on the water, he wet a cloth and handed it to her. After several minutes, she managed to get herself under control. Leaning against the sink, her head lowered as she tried to think of what to do next.

"Do you need to use the bathroom?" His husky voice drew her back to the present.

"Yes, thanks."

He went out the door, closing it behind him. It was that infinitesimal action that had her finally realizing that she was safe.

Sawyer came out of the bathroom thinking that she was never going to take that privilege for granted again. If her mother were still alive, she would point out that the danger she had been in was her own fault, and how it could have been prevented if she had been smart enough not to trust anyone.

Her mother had always been afraid every time Sawyer

had left home, whether it was to go to school or outside to play. *You have to be careful*, she would tell her over and over. She could just hear her saying *I told you so* in her mind.

Sawyer went back into the other room, and heard one of the men talking to Kaden.

"What in the hell are we going to do with them?"

"Sin, give me a minute to think," Kaden snapped.

"This is going to blow up all over the tabloids," the one Kaden had called R.J. said, pacing the room.

"Shut up, R.J. This is all your fucking fault," Alec said, taking the phone away from his mouth long enough to make the statement before turning his back to the room and continuing his conversation.

The group of women she had been brought in with were huddled together on one of the couches, watching the men anxiously, waiting to see what the men were going to do. None of them took the incentive to save themselves. Sawyer was sure it had been beaten out of them.

Fuck that. Sawyer knew exactly what she was going to do.

"Give me a phone," Sawyer said, walking further into the room.

Everyone turned to her.

"Who are you going to call?" Kaden and R.J. both spoke at the same time.

"The police," Sawyer stated, holding out her hand.

"Did you not hear what he said?" one of the men said as he rose from the couch. "He has Ax."

"Sin," Kaden warned before turning to look directly at her. "What's your name?"

"Sawyer," she supplied her name reluctantly. "Sawyer Bennett."

"Sawyer, before we call anyone, we're going to figure out our best options for everyone's safety."

"Our only option is to call the police," she protested.

"Do you think your friend, Vida, would agree?" At his

words, Sawyer remained silent. She needed a phone to call Vida to warn her to hide. "I need to call her to warn her."

Kaden pulled a phone out of his pocket. "What's her number?"

Sawyer's mouth dropped open. Deciding it was better to call Vida first then argue with Kaden and the others later, she gave him the number. He let it ring several minutes before disconnecting the call.

"She didn't answer," Kaden said unnecessarily.

Sawyer's mind went into panic mode for her friend's safety. She started for the door only to be stopped by Kaden and Alec, who hurriedly finished his conversation.

"Listen to me, Sawyer," Alec started.

"G—g—get out of m—my way!" Sawyer screamed, trying to get by the two men preventing her from leaving. When the dark haired man named Sin and the other men in the room also moved to block her path, she knew it was useless. "I can't believe that you're stopping me from getting help," Sawyer said in frustration. "Your friend is in danger, too. Don't you care?"

"Yes. That's why we need to decide what to do before we make a move. Rushing and calling the police might get him killed," Kaden tried to reason with her, but it was his next words that had her actually listening.

"It wasn't the police who found you, Sawyer. It was me, and the fact that Alec was smart enough to realize something wasn't right. Do you think that your disappearance was reported to the police? Did they come in rushing to save you? No. We are trying to protect them," he pointed to the women huddled on the couch, "as well as you. We're concerned for our friend's safety as you are for Vida's. We have resources that would be effective if you would just listen and give us an opportunity to get situated."

Kaden's hard voice brought her to the decision that she would listen for now, then find a way to call for help later. She would let them think she was giving in if it would give her time to get away.

"I've called in my security team, which would have already been here if R.J. hadn't held them up downstairs in the lobby."

"They had to be checked out," R.J. said stubbornly.

"You dumb fuck, if you hadn't done that, they would have been up here before Redman and his men showed up." Alec took a deep breath. "A couple of my men were on the police force, another is a computer expert, and three of them are special ops. My team is able to deal with Redman and get Ax back, but I can't keep getting diverted by you and the others." He looked at Kaden.

"Do what you have to do. I trust your judgment," Kaden told Alec.

"How am I not surprised?" Sawyer said sarcastically. "The p—problem is for some reason you guys are more concerned with keeping this quiet than getting p—professional help. Who are you anyway?" Sawyer studied the men in the room, not recognizing any of them. She didn't think they were sports figures. The men in the room looked fit and muscular, but they weren't wide or tall enough for basketball or football players.

The man sitting on the couch, who up to this point had remained silent, looked at her as if she were an alien. "We're Mouth2Mouth. Haven't you heard of us?" He pointed to Kaden. "That's Kaden Cross."

Sawyer searched her memory and could find no memory of the group or of Kaden's name. That wasn't unusual; her mother hadn't let her listen to music while she was growing up, and even after she had finished high school, her mother had guilt tripped her into remaining home until she had been murdered one day coming home from work.

"I'm D-mon." He pointed to the dark haired man leaning against the wall. "That's Sin. R.J. is our tour manager. Ax was the one Redman took."

"I'm sorry. I've never heard of you. I'm not into music

31

much." Sawyer could tell her lack of recognition didn't hurt their egos when they were all studying her as if she would suddenly recognize them.

She saw Kaden's mouth twitch in amusement at her last sentence. All the room stared at her in dismay. Even the other women looked at her in pity. She and Vida lived a quiet life; neither of them had been into partying. Vida spent all her free time studying, while her own time had been spent working to support her friend so she could finish her degree.

The door opened, and men began pouring into the room. Sawyer took a step back before she realized that these were the extra security that Alec had been talking about. He talked with them and Kaden while she took a seat on one of the empty chairs.

Her stomach grumbled and the women turned to stare at her. Blushing, she crossed her arms over her stomach, hoping to silence the embarrassing noise.

Kaden was watching her, and at her revealing movement, he turned his attention to Sin.

"Call and have some food and drinks sent up here." Sin nodded, catching the cell phone that Kaden tossed toward him. The men talked for what seemed like forever to her tense nerves, but Sawyer reminded herself to be patient. She already had decided to ask who brought up the food for help.

Her plans were derailed when one of Alec's men went to the door, wheeling in the trolley filled with food himself, leaving the server outside in the hallway.

As the women and men descended on the food cart, Sawyer's stomach lurched at the aroma coming from it, but she couldn't bring herself to eat while she was so worried about Vida and wanting to call for help.

Finally, when the men finished talking, Alec and his security team left with grim faces.

Sawyer watched as Kaden walked over to the food cart where he placed several sandwiches on a plate and grabbed a bottled water before walking over, handing it to her.

"Eat," he ordered. She started to argue with him, but her grumbling stomach refused to cooperate. Embarrassed, she reached out and took the plate from his hand.

"So what have you and Alec decided?" Sawyer asked, before taking a bite of the thick sandwich.

Kaden sat down on the chair facing hers.

"Alec is going to find a safe place for the women to stay. Two of Alec's security detail that used to be on the police force are going to get in touch with their ex-bosses and bring them in quietly so as not to alarm Redman and whoever his boss is. We're going to hang tight until we hear back from Alec."

"In other words, you're not going to do a damn thing. None of this wait-and-see attitude is going to prevent them from going after my friend." Sawyer had to force herself to take another bite. His words making her appetite dwindle.

"Alec is tracing the number you dialed and is going to keep trying it. If we don't get in touch with her soon, then we'll send one of our men to where she is to get her out of town."

Sawyer ate the sandwich, enjoying the taste despite herself. The thick sandwich was filled with a flavorful meat that had her reaching for another one. After she finished it and drank half her bottled water, she sat, debating her next move.

Alec returned and asked the women to follow him after a quiet conversation with Kaden. The women meekly followed him out of the hotel room.

"Where is he taking them?" Sawyer asked, concerned for their safety.

Kaden returned his attention to her. "He's taking them to a private rehab home not far from here. They'll be checked out and given help to get rid of the drugs Redman has kept in their systems.

Rehab houses were known for their discretion and silence dealing with wealthy clients. These women weren't being given their freedom, but exchanging it for a more luxurious prison.

"Why aren't you trying to send me with them?" she asked suspiciously.

"Because Redman wants you; he doesn't want them."

His words had what little color the food had given her disappearing again. Did that mean he had decided to give her back to Rick? The door had been unintentionally left open after the last woman had left the suite.

"I need to go to the restroom." Nonchalantly, she rose to her feet.

"Fine." Kaden was motioned to Sin's and R.J.'s side after he'd dismissed her.

Sawyer turned toward the bathroom, and before anyone could react, she ran for the door. She saw the elevator door was closed, so seeing the exit sign and hearing running steps and yells from behind her, she went for the exit.

Her movements were slow after being chained to a bed for several weeks, but she managed to make it to the door. Her hands touched the knob, frantically turning the handle and barreling through the door only to find herself almost knocked off her feet when she ran into one of Alec's men coming up the stairs. His hands went to her waist, barely managing to keep them from both going headfirst down the steps.

"Jesus," Kaden said, his arm going to her waist and pulling them both back to safety.

The security man released her with a sharp word while Kaden gripped her arm, forcing her struggling body back into the hotel room. The band members and R.J. all gave her angry stares at her attempt to escape.

Kaden didn't stop escorting her down the hallway where he opened the bedroom door, then pushed her in before she could stop him, shutting and locking the door before she could react.

"S—s—son of a b—bitch!" Sawyer turned and began hitting the door with her fists, yelling to be let out. Trying the door handle, she realized the lock was strong, and she wasn't going to be able to break out anytime soon. Pounding on the door, she continued to yell for help, hoping fruitlessly that someone would hear and come to her aid. When her voice gave out, and her burning fists couldn't take it anymore, she slid down the door, sitting on the floor and leaning back against the door for support.

"I'm sorry," she heard Kaden mutter from the other side of the door, before his footsteps sounded, leading away from the door.

She was being held captive again, losing her freedom before she actually had regained it. A self-mocking laugh escaped her lips. As always, freedom was just beyond her reach.

Chapter Five

"Kaden you should see the turkey Mom bought. It's so big it won't fit in the oven."

"How many pounds?" Kaden asked Grace, watching Tatiana trying on the lingerie they had spent the morning shopping for.

"At least twenty-four. I don't know how she's going to make it fit in the oven." Her soft laughter came through the phone with a slight edge to the sound. "I thought you would have been on your way. You said you were leaving yesterday."

"Yeah, well, something's come up. We're not going to be able to come. Tatiana's parents are throwing a fit that she's not coming home for Thanksgiving, so we're going to have to go there. It's important to them since we just got engaged. Mom will understand."

"Kaden, she's been cooking for the last two days." Disappointment filled her voice, which he ignored as Tatiana struck a pose in her new, red lace camisole. She hadn't bothered to put on the flimsy bottoms.

"I'll make it up to her. We'll spend a few extra days at Christmas. I have to go, Grace. Tell everyone, hi."

Smiling, Tatiana took the phone away as her arms circled his neck, disconnecting the call.

Kaden sat on the leather chair, looking out the tinted tour bus window, watching the scenery as they drove toward their next concert venue. The silence in the forty-five-foot bus was strained.

His return to the band was turning out to be one fucked up mess. They had spent the previous day trying to figure a way out of the mess they had found themselves in, while Sawyer had tried to contact her friend with no success. Each time he had gone into the bedroom to give her the phone, her look of reproach had him regretting his decision not to go to the police. It was only his faith in Alec's ability to handle the situation that had him keeping the woman contained.

Alec took the chair next to his. "We have a problem."

"No shit. Which problem are you talking about? A pimp threatening us, the fact that we've kidnapped Sawyer or the failure to notify the police about a crime?" Kaden said sarcastically.

"The police know, or rather the FBI. One of my men has a contact in the FBI. He told them what happened. Kaden, if it wasn't for your quick thinking none of us would be here today. Redman works for a highly dangerous man named Digger, who has been running a sex ring for years. The FBI has been building a case to arrest him, but they haven't been able to locate where he keeps the women. It seems that he has a way of making them disappear, and they don't show back up again; at least, not alive." Alec's grim visage showed the extreme danger they were all in.

"Jesus," Kaden said, still thankful that Redman had returned this morning with Ax when the money had cleared his account.

All the men stood around the bus, listening as Alec explained the tenuous situation.

"They've put the women in the rehab center in protective custody, but are leaving them there. None of them are talking; they're too afraid of this Digger to give

37

evidence."

"What about Sawyer?" Kaden asked. "Should we turn her over to the FBI?" He still remembered Redman's final words when Ax was returned that morning.

"*You better keep that bitch under control. Any escape attempts and I'll either blow her brains out or take her back. Either way, she won't be around to play those games you kept your other bitches playing.*"

Alec's voice drew him back to the present. "They want us to keep doing what we're doing. They've placed an undercover agent in with my security, and they're keeping us under surveillance. The FBI are hoping that this Digger will make a move on Sawyer and they can finally get some evidence on him."

"Why not just get Sawyer to testify? She doesn't seem the type to be afraid to testify." She would probably demand to testify if given the chance.

"The problem is that she can't testify against Digger because she's never seen him. He's the one they want. Arresting Redman, would slow the operation down, not eliminate it and find the missing women."

The only choice was to keep Sawyer, if there was any chance to find the other women. Kaden sighed; they weren't going to be able to leave this problem behind. They were going to have to stick it out.

"I'll tell Sawyer that…" Kaden began.

"She can't know. The FBI says if she is taken, despite their efforts, that she could be forced to tell them what she knows, and Digger and his men will disappear. They say the least she knows, the better, for her own safety."

Kaden didn't agree, especially if it would take that accusing look out of her eyes. He also didn't think they were taking Sawyer's safety seriously if they were more concerned with arresting Digger.

"So what's the problem you're talking about?" Kaden asked Alec.

"Another reason they don't want us to tell Sawyer is

her connection to another man named King. They think that was the original reason she was kidnapped."

"How does she know this King?" The fragile woman appeared to have a few secrets.

"No one knows. Digger is trying to move into King's territory and Digger intends to use Sawyer against him, but no one knows how. As far as the FBI can find, they didn't even know each other. The only thing that tied King to her is a protection order he put out years ago for her and her friend, Vida."

"Can this become anymore of a clusterfuck?" Kaden said angrily, getting to his feet to move around the bus. As large as it was, he was starting to feel smothered in the confining space, surrounded by the listening band members.

"I'm sorry. This is all my fault. I thought I was saving everyone from the press. Instead, everyone's in danger. I didn't know the women were from a slave ring. I thought they were just doing it for the money." R.J. sat at the table, drinking a glass of whiskey, his face pale.

"You should have learned by now that it never works out when you interfere," Kaden said angrily, before asking Alec about Sawyer's friend.

"Does Vida know that she's in danger?"

Alec nodded his head. "She's a smart girl. She went to King for protection. The FBI thinks she's safe and are watching her also."

"They want to take both Digger and King down using those girls, don't they?" Kaden questioned.

"Yes," Alec answered.

"Fuck."

"What are we going to do?" Ax asked. He was sitting at the table with R.J., but had a bottle of whiskey, and Kaden couldn't blame him. If not for his own self-imposed ban against alcohol, he would have the whole bottle in front of him by now.

"The only thing we can do is what the FBI wants us to

do. Keep Sawyer safe until they can arrest this Digger," Kaden stated, coming to the same conclusion he'd seen in Alec's eyes.

"She's not going to be happy about that," D-mon said, nodding to the bedroom door.

"She might hate us, but she'll be alive," Kaden said grimly.

Kaden heated several of the premade meals for the men in the microwave. When it was done, he made a plate for Sawyer and picked up a beer and bottled water, taking everything to the bedroom at the back of the bus. It was his when they were on tour, but they had locked her up inside to keep her from distracting the driver while the bus was moving.

Alec unlocked the door for him before going to make himself a plate of food. Kaden went into the dark bedroom where he saw Sawyer curled up on the bed, still in the same clothes she had been wearing when he had found her in the hotel room. The hoodie had been thrown to the floor.

Kaden managed to set the food down on the desk before turning on the light.

"Why are you sitting here in the dark?"

She didn't answer him; she merely laid her cheek down on her knees as she silently watched him. Kaden shoved his hands into his jean's pockets, staring at the woman sitting on his bed.

"You'll feel better if you take a shower and change your clothes." Again he tried unsuccessfully to interact with the silent woman. His guilty conscience wouldn't let him talk harshly with her, but it was going against his grain to pacify a woman who was ignoring him. Usually, he just told them what to do, and they jumped, wanting to make him happy. Even the few women he had been with after he had stepped out of the limelight had wanted to please him.

"You can't escape if you don't keep your strength up." Her golden eyes stared at him before she angrily climbed off the bed, moving toward the desk and pulling the chair out. She then ignored him as she started to eat the food. Opening the water, she took a long drink.

Kaden was wary to say anything in case she would stop eating. Unable to prevent himself, though, he took a seat on the bottom edge of the bed. "How did Redman kidnap you?"

She swallowed a bite of food in her mouth before answering his question. "H—he came into the restaurant I was working at; several of the workers knew him. He asked me out a couple of times, but I turned him down. Then he offered me dinner at a five star restaurant I couldn't afford, so finally I said y—yes." Her lips twisted in self-disgust. "We left my apartment and that's the last thing I remember until I woke up in that r—room with the women.

"I—I would have still been there if Redman hadn't needed one more woman for you and your friends, and the other women were in too bad of shape, physically."

The disgust she made no effort to hide had him getting to his feet. "We didn't hire those women. Our tour manager screwed up, but neither me nor the guys in the band knew the women weren't willing."

"Oh, they were willing. The drugs Rick gave them made sure of that."

Kaden winced at her words. "I know you're angry, Sawyer, and I can't blame you. I can only assure you we mean you no harm." Standing up, seeing she was finished, he took her plate and the beer bottle she hadn't touched. "The other women are safe, and as soon as Alec thinks it's safe to release you, we will."

"What about my friend, Vida?"

"She's still not answering her phone," Kaden lied. Alec had said that she was under King's protection now, and the FBI thought that the women shouldn't be able to talk. They didn't want Vida running before they had a case against King. Both women were being used as pawns and

Kaden had a feeling one or both of them were going to end up hurt.

Sawyer searched his eyes, but Kaden was an experienced liar and knew how to hide the truth from a woman. Going to the door, he opened it before her next words had him unexpectedly turning back.

"You're lying."

Her perceptive response had him startled. "Take a shower, Sawyer. Get changed." He refused to acknowledge that he hadn't told the whole truth.

"Go fuck yourself," she said, throwing the half full water bottle at his head, which made him almost drop the plate and beer bottle he was holding.

Seeing the temper the woman was capable of, his dominant blood stirred, wanting to tame her; however, he forced down the desire, giving her a hard stare that more than one woman knew to be wary of. Kaden had never found pleasure in getting submission from someone naturally submissive. Instead, he thrived on the challenge of obtaining submission from a strong woman who gave in to his demands, wanting the pleasure he could give her.

"I'm trying to be a nice guy here, Sawyer. Under the circumstances, I can understand your anger, but if you use physical violence against me again, don't expect me to stand still and take it without consequences." Kaden let his words hang in the air as he went out the door, closing and locking it behind him.

Chapter Six

Sawyer stood backstage in the VIP room. Kaden had let her out of the bus to watch the concert they were to perform. She didn't even know which city they were in, since she the bus's movements had lulled her to sleep last night.

The large room was filled with the band members as they waited to be called to the stage, Sawyer presumed. She had expected them to change their clothes for their performances, but they hadn't, staying in their casual jeans and t-shirts instead.

The room was filled with different bottles of liquor, water and sodas, while food trays sat around as they each took their turn snacking on the vast array available to them. Sawyer, having worked in several restaurants that catered, knew the money that went into fixing the table with their smorgasbord of luxury items.

"Hungry?" Ax asked. Sawyer shook her head in response. He was the friendliest of the men. He was constantly trying to talk to her and give her reassurance that everything would be fine. She thought it was his own recent journey into Rick's world that had him so sensitive to her situation.

Kaden, she had noticed, had taken a seat away from the others, getting up every so often to move around the room without talking to any of the other men.

"He goes into his own head right before a performance," Ax said, taking a beer from the ice bucket. Sawyer's eyes went to the television screen in the room where they could see the stage. A group was out there amping up the atmosphere until Mouth2Mouth was to take the stage.

"They're pretty good. They're new, but they'll make it eventually, especially if they keep writing the songs the way their fans like."

Sawyer nodded her head, listening to the soulful voice of the woman singing on the stage. She commanded the stage with her vitality and voice, drawing the crowd into a round of applause when her song ended.

"It's time," R.J. said from the doorway.

"Hell, yeah! Let's do this," Ax yelled, and Sawyer felt her lips twitch in a smile for the first time since Rick had kidnapped her.

The men filed out of the room, slapping each other on the back.

Kaden stopped in front of her. "Behave, Sawyer." He didn't wait for her to tell him to fuck off again. He simply left her with an infectious grin that she was hard-pressed not to return.

She was now the only one left in the room except for Alec, who remained by the door. "Relax, Sawyer. Enjoy the show."

Frustrated, Sawyer took a seat on the expensive couch, watching as all of the men ran onto the stage, except for Kaden. Her eyes searched, but she didn't see him. She did hear his voice, though. Soft, yet strong, he sang the words as the stage lights gradually lifted, finding him sitting on the corner of the stage with a guitar. His voice immediately drew her in and didn't let go. He moved around the stage, commanding the audience's attention as he played the guitar.

Sawyer swallowed. Jeez, the man had sex appeal in spades. You could actually feel the sexually suggestive song in your bones as if he was singing it just to her. Sawyer tried to draw herself out of the music, but couldn't. Only when the song ended did she move her eyes away from the screen. He wasn't finished, going from one song to the next flawlessly, but she didn't allow herself to become trapped in the spell he was casting over his audience.

The band was the perfect foil for him. Each with their own talented skills, they had the audience divided as to who was the more talented. They blended their music and voices into songs that went from heart wrenching to full on rock, and had the audience dancing and singing along.

"He's very good," Sawyer reluctantly admitted.

"He's more than good," Alec replied. "He was world famous when he gave the business up five years ago. He has the talent to become a legend."

Sawyer had to agree, watching him. "Why did he leave?" Doubtful that if he was as big as Alec said that he would willingly walk away.

Alec couldn't hide his surprise. "You really don't know?"

Sawyer shook her head.

"It made all the tabloids. He went into rehab for six months, and when he came out, he never returned to the stage. His backup singer, Jesse, took over. They've done well performing his songs, but nothing like the crowd out there now. Only half those seats had been sold until they heard that Kaden was returning; then they sold out."

Kaden removed his t-shirt on the stage and Sawyer's mouth almost dropped open. His body had several tattoos on his chest and back. She had seen the ones on his arms; those were hard to miss, but the ones that covered his chest and back rocked the sexuality of his movements on the stage up a few degrees. Even Sawyer felt her body react to his sensuality, and she'd told herself that she hated the man.

"He doesn't seem the type to let anything control him." Sawyer turned away from the screen, noticing Alec didn't say anything.

"How did you meet Kaden?" Sawyer asked, going to the table to reach for one of the sparkling waters and one of the tiny sandwiches before going to the couch and nibbling on the sandwich.

"In rehab."

She had thought that he had known Kaden from before. "It doesn't bother you being around the band drinking?" Sawyer regretted her words as soon as they left her lips. She had never been insensitive or rude before her kidnapping. She forced herself to swallow the small bite of sandwich in her mouth. "I'm sorry. That was rude of me."

Alec studied her several seconds before he replied, "Alcohol wasn't my problem. Kaden made it a condition of his return that no drugs were going to be permitted on this tour."

"Alcohol must not have been Kaden's weakness either then."

"I don't think Kaden has a weakness anymore," Alec replied.

Sawyer picked up one of the magazines, ignoring the screen for the rest of the concert. She only looked up when she heard Kaden's voice blend with a female voice. She reluctantly found herself watching as Kaden sang a song with the lead singer of the backup band. Her body constantly rubbed against his as they sang. Each time, the crowd got louder and louder.

"Did she tour with Kaden before he left?"

"No. From my understanding, they find a new band every tour," Alec told her as he watched the two interact on the stage.

Sawyer turned her attention away, not wanting to watch the two together, without being sure why. She hated

Kaden for not letting her contact the police or to warn Vida. Sawyer got up from the couch at the thought of her friend, becoming restless.

"How much longer?"

"They're finishing up now."

She half-listened and half-brooded as they did two more songs before leaving the stage. When they didn't return to the room, she looked at Alec.

"Encore." Just as he explained, the band returned for three more songs before finally giving their goodbyes to the applauding crowd.

The band returned to the VIP room; their energy bouncing off the walls. Alec took her arm, seating her in a chair, unobtrusively out of the way, as several fans were allowed in the room to take pictures with the band members.

Sawyer saw Kaden talking to a man with a recorder as she watched everyone in the room. Slowly realizing that it was the press, she started to rise out of her chair.

A hard hand on her shoulder pressed her back down into her seat. "Don't, Sawyer. I'll pack you out of here to the bus before you can say anything and Kaden will just tell everyone that you were overwhelmed coming so close to him."

Sawyer bit her lip, debating her chance of success. She didn't want to be trapped in the bus during the concerts they performed. She couldn't escape from the secure bus. Her only chance was during these concerts. She was going to have to play it smart and lull them into a false sense of security. They had two more concerts this week; a better chance would surely become available.

When Kaden went to the table, grabbing a bottled water, Sawyer watched as he drank the bottle. He still hadn't put his shirt back on. The lead singer from the other band came into the room with her band following, each of them laughing and talking familiarly with Kaden's band.

The woman singer went to Kaden, who was still standing at the table. Her arm circling his waist as she pressed herself against him, whispering into his ear. Sawyer tore her eyes away, not having to guess what the woman was saying to him. When she had worked at the restaurant, she'd served at the bar. She had seen women letting men know when they were available numerous times, and that was exactly what the woman was doing.

Feeling Alec watching her, she moved her attention toward the others. Sin was talking to one of the women who had a backstage pass. His dark hair was tumbled, but his face was lit up with excitement. All the men had the same expression on their faces; however, Ax and D-mon were both antsy, roaming the room. Sawyer thought the excitement of the show, stoking the audience, had left them feeling a rush; it was probably hard to come down from.

People came and went as the band took turns signing autographs and taking pictures. Becoming bored, Sawyer stood up.

"It's almost over; another ten minutes and we'll go back to the bus," Alec informed her. Going back to the confining space of the bus was nothing to look forward to, she thought.

"I need to go to the restroom."

"Through that door." Alec pointed to the doorway at the back of the room, but he didn't make a move to follow her toward the restroom. Disappointed, Sawyer came to the conclusion that there must not be a way for her to sneak out.

Going through the doorway, she saw the restroom door to the left. Opening the door, she came to a stop. Sin had a woman pressed up against the wall, her lower body bared and her skirt pulled to her waist as he fucked her. Both of them turned toward her, hearing her gasp. Hastily, her face flaming in embarrassment, she stepped back out, closing the door quickly. Rushing back out into the

48

crowded room, she resumed her seat, feeling several curious eyes on her.

"That was quick," Alec said, returning to her side.

"It was occupied." His eyes narrowed on her before an amused smile played across his lips. His eyes searched the room before coming back to hers.

"I take it Sin was getting better acquainted with one of the locals?"

Sawyer gave a brief nod, twisting her hands together, and then looked away at his amusement and found her eyes caught by Kaden's. The woman was still hanging onto him, but her smile appeared more forced.

"Let's go," Alec said, taking her arm. Sawyer didn't argue, wanting to get away from the embarrassing situation and Kaden's watchful eyes.

The hallway was busy with fans and workers moving around. Alec led her to a series of heavy doors before coming to a set of double steel doors where she recognized two of his men who opened them. Hurriedly, he maneuvered her through the crowd with determination, not letting any of the fans jostle her. Sawyer thought of jerking away and making a run for it, but almost as if he read her mind, his hand tightened on her arm, propelling her forward. Before she could come up with another plan, she found herself back on the bus.

"Do you want to sit in here or go back into the bedroom?"

At least he gave me a choice, she thought sarcastically, but not wanting to face Sin so soon after getting a bird's eye view of his cock, she was ready to go back into the bedroom.

Without answering him, she moved toward the back of the bus, going inside the room. She heard the lock behind her when the door closed. Regretting not being able to think of a way to escape, she felt like a failure letting Vida down.

Hearing the door unlock then open later, she looked

toward it, seeing Kaden come into the bedroom.

"The other shower is busy," he explained his presence.

"Help yourself," Sawyer said, waving her hand toward the bathroom.

His lips quirked at her giving him permission to use his own bathroom. She watched as he went to the closet and pulled out his bag, removing clothing before going into the bathroom. Sawyer then turned on the television to drown out the sound of him in the shower. Her imagination saw him removing his clothes and stepping into the surprisingly large shower.

Twining a lock of her hair around her finger, she forced herself to choose a program as she felt the bus begin to move. She didn't ask where they were going next, because she knew it was taking her further and further away from Vida.

Sawyer's eyes grew heavy and she lay down on her side, curling comfortably into the mattress. It was sometime later, when the bathroom door opened, that she was jerked awake.

"Do you need anything?"

"You could stop the bus and let me off," she said, sitting up.

His lips tightened. "I was talking about something to eat or drink."

"I know what you meant," Sawyer snapped. "How long are you going to do this, Kaden? You're holding me prisoner against my will. Eventually you'll have to let me go, and then you and your entire band are going to go to jail," she said angrily.

"I don't think it's too smart telling me that, do you?" Kaden crossed his arms over his chest, watching her reaction.

Sawyer forced herself not to let his attitude intimidate her. "Let me go, Kaden, and I won't say a thing to the police. I promise." Sawyer meant it; she just wanted her freedom. She would tell the police about the other women, but she would keep Kaden and his band out of it if he would let her go.

"Somehow, I just don't believe you, Sawyer." When she opened her mouth to explain, he cut her off. "Sawyer, I told you what Redman said. I'm keeping you for you and your friend's safety."

"I don't need your help." At his look of disbelief, she corrected herself. "I just want to get Vida and disappear."

"How? You said you worked as a waitress; how are you just going to disappear from a group of men involved in a sex ring who want you dead?"

Sawyer winced at his blunt words.

"V—Vida and I have been saving. We have almost five thousand dollars..." She turned red. She was aware five thousand wasn't a large sum of money to him, but it was a fortune to her and Vida.

"Five thousand isn't going to be enough to hide you from men like Redman. They'll have you in a week. This time, they'll have your friend, Vida, also. It will take weeks, if not months, for the police to build a case. As soon as you tried to get a job when your money ran out, they would have you."

She hadn't thought of that, assuming that the police would make an immediate arrest. She had heard that it took time to gather evidence and prosecute criminals; however, she hadn't thought about it in regards to her and Vida's safety. She was going to have to start thinking smarter if they stood any chance of surviving.

Chapter Seven

Sawyer sat in the corner, watching another after party, and at the same time, wanting to scream in frustration as yet another woman slipped unnoticed into the room. How so many could sneak into the guarded room while she couldn't slip out was working her nerves to a screaming point.

Being constantly monitored by Kaden and Alec, plus being on the bus, was bringing back the memories of her childhood where her over-protective mother had smothered her with attention after the death of her father.

It had been three weeks since she had begun being held prisoner by Kaden. At first, she'd tried to remain aloof from the band, but the individual band members were gradually wearing down her intentions. She was deathly afraid that they were weakening her resolve to escape.

Ax especially was sweet toward her, with a sense of humor that never failed to get a reluctant smile from her. He drove the other band members crazy with his pranks, and Sawyer especially enjoyed it when Kaden was the victim. He had locked Kaden inside his bed compartment with the sliding door this morning, and swore he didn't remember where he had put the key.

She had sat at the kitchen table, smirking into her coffee as she wondered how he liked a dose of his own medicine when Alec had spoilt the fun by picking the lock and releasing a furious Kaden. He had gone for the prankster and wrestled him from one end of the bus to the other. At first she had thought that Ax would be the easy winner of the wrestling match with his larger, muscled frame, but Kaden had quickly changed her opinion. Kaden may be lean; however, he was a dirtier fighter.

Alec's attention was diverted by a curvy brunette, who was flirting with him, while Kaden was surrounded by at least two women. Sin had disappeared for his concert hump, and D-mon, as usual, had his own personal fan club vying for his attention.

Sawyer nonchalantly got to her feet as if going to get a drink. Using the crowd as cover, she edged for the door. A number of women came in the door and Sawyer took the opportunity to slide through. She saw Alec's men with their backs turned, trying to keep the large number of women back. This arena was larger than the previous ones, with more exits for the men to cover, and they were becoming overwhelmed.

Not hesitating, she used the forward momentum of a large group of women to slip into the crowd.

"Hey! Stop!" one of the security detail yelled.

Frantically, knowing she had been seen, she weaved through the crowd, which she now realized had a number of men. Seeing a group of males, she smiled and edged in between them, hoping their height would hide her while she figured out which direction to go. She saw Alec and D-mon rushed past and shrunk down.

One of the men was looking down at her curiously. Expecting him to question her, he gave her a wink and slung his arm over her shoulder. "Get to rowdy for you, sweet thing?"

It dawned on Sawyer that they thought she was

frightened of the crowd.

"Yes," she mumbled, looking around.

"Stay by me; I'll keep you safe," the young man bragged, without a muscle on the arm around her shoulders to back up his boastful words.

His friends laughed. Seeing an exit sign, she was about to take off again when his arm tightened around her shoulder. "Where you going? Stay. We're going to party after they leave. You can keep us company."

Sawyer didn't feel afraid, not even when his hand went to her ass, bringing her up to his side.

Sin and D-mon walked by, searching through the crowd.

"Sounds good." Sawyer would agree to anything to get out of the arena. She could ditch them when she managed to get outside.

"Let her go," Kaden's voice sounded from behind her back.

"Go find yourself your own woman. Take your pick. The whole place is full of them," he joked, making his buddies laugh.

"The one that I want has your hand on her ass," Kaden said sharply. The man removed his hand from her ass, drawing his fist back. Kaden looked back at the man, daring him to make a move.

"It's Kaden Cross," she yelled, drawing attention to their group.

Kaden gave her a sharp glance, while the man about to clock Kaden, looked around in surprise just before the crowd surged around them. Using the opportunity, Sawyer again slipped through the surging crowd. She felt guilty when D-mon and Sin were recognized as well and were swarmed in a mass of female bodies. The guards watching the doors moved forward, trying to rescue Kaden, D-mon and Sin.

Sawyer opened the heavy door, running through it, but came to a halt when she was grabbed from behind.

Looking back, she saw it was Ax who had stopped her flight.

"P—p—please, Ax. L—let me go." She could tell he was wavering on his choice of releasing her or not. Gratefully, she took a step forward only to have her shoulder caught in Alec's tight grip.

"That was stupid, Sawyer. You could have gotten someone hurt. My men are still trying to get Kaden out." Grimly, he propelled her toward the parked bus. The crowd thinned out as he drew closer to it. Angrily rapping on the door, he threw her a disgusted look as it swung open.

One of Alec's men reached down as Alec shoved her unceremoniously forward.

"Take her and lock her in the bedroom. I have to get Kaden." Alec's man drew her up the step, leaving her no choice as he rushed her to the bedroom where he unapologetically pushed her inside before locking the door.

Sawyer stood, staring at the door, biting her trembling lip. She refused to feel guilty for alerting the crowd to the fact that Kaden was there. She'd had to take a chance to escape and get to Vida, didn't she?

She stood there several moments not knowing what to do, when she heard a loud crash against the door. Frightened, Sawyer took a step back from the door, listening to what she thought was a struggle. Loud voices were muted against the door. She had learned through talking to Ax that the bedroom was soundproof, so whoever was sleeping wouldn't be disturbed by what was happening in the front of the bus. Sawyer waited anxiously for Kaden to storm into the room, so it was almost anticlimactic to hear the low voices retreat.

Sawyer went to sit on the bottom of the bed, feeling the bus start and begin moving. She twined a curl of hair around her finger over and over. She'd had the fixation since she was a little girl. She had almost broken the habit, yet recently, she seemed to be doing it constantly.

She tensed when she heard the key in the door, and then held her breath as it swung inward, presenting Kaden standing in the doorway. Her first glance at him almost had her jumping up to run to the safety of the bathroom and locking herself in, but she doubted she would make it from the deadly stare Kaden was focusing on her.

She wanted to look away, although she didn't; her guilt forcing her to accept the blame for his condition. His nose was swollen and bloody, and his hair was a mess with several spots having blood matting it down. There were numerous scratch marks on his face, and even on his chest, which she could see through the tattered remains of his t-shirt.

"Oh!"

Kaden's lips tightened at her response. "You fucking bitch." Kaden strode forward. "Seven people are being sent to the hospital because of your stunt." Jerking her to her feet, he propelled her into the bathroom, slamming the door closed behind them.

"I didn't mean for anyone to get hurt." Sawyer fought back the tears threatening to escape. She bit back a sob when she saw that several of the scratches were deep.

"You don't care about anybody but yourself, Sawyer," Kaden said harshly, pulling out a first aid kit from the small closet, slamming it down on the bathroom counter.

"That's not true," Sawyer protested.

"Yes, it is. Alec saw one of Redman's men in the crowd. Even if you had managed to get outside the arena, he would have had you within minutes."

Sawyer paled. She had been so focused on escaping Alec's security; she hadn't given a thought to Rick's men possibly being so close.

Kaden closed the lid to the toilet, taking a seat. "You can clean me up since you're the reason I got hurt." She started to refuse, but thought for her own safety that it was better to concede to his demands.

Going to the counter, she pulled out some antiseptic and cotton balls, which she dabbed with the antiseptic before hesitantly moving closer to him. He had flung the remains of his t-shirt into the laundry basket before glaring up at her. Gently she cleaned the scratches on his face and then got a clean one to do his chest. She winced when she saw how deep it was, taking her time to make sure that it was clean. She smeared antibiotic ointment onto each of the scratches. Tilting his head back, she then cleaned his bloody nose with a wet cloth, forcing herself to continue when more blood oozed out. Finally, the bleeding stopped and she began to sanitize the cuts on his head, which took several minutes to clean as she realized several handfuls of his hair had been pulled out by the roots.

"I—I g—guess you're more popular than I realized," she tried to wisecrack, inwardly sickened by the sight of his scalp.

"Sawyer, I don't know how, but in some way you have mistakenly come to the conclusion that I'm a nice guy," Kaden spoke from between his clenched teeth.

"N—no I didn't," Sawyer interrupted.

"You do or you wouldn't be standing there, making lame ass jokes at my expense."

Kaden stood up and Sawyer took a step back, going to the first aid kit and putting everything back in order. She glanced up to see that Kaden was undressing behind her.

"What are you doing?"

"I'm going to take a shower," Kaden replied, unsnapping his jeans. With a gasp, Sawyer fled the bathroom, slamming the door shut behind her.

She turned on the television and took a seat in the chair by the window. She had made the mistake in trying to escape before thinking it through. Not only her safety was at stake; Vida's was as well. She stared out the dark window, thinking about her friend, wishing she was there to talk to. They had always confided everything with each other, ever since they were little.

The bathroom door opening drew her attention as Kaden came out with just a towel wrapped around his hips. His dark hair was wet and his lean body still had droplets of water sliding down his chest to be caught by the towel. Sawyer swallowed at the man's overt sensuality and lack of modesty, while he ignored her, going to the closet to pull out his bag, taking out fresh clothes.

"I'm sorry."

Her husky voice had him pausing before he zipped his bag closed. Tossing the towel to the floor, he unconcernedly put on his jeans. Sawyer turned her head away, listening to the rustle of his clothes as he dressed.

"Come here."

Sawyer's head turned to see that he was standing in the middle of the floor with his hands tucked into his pockets. She was determined to stay seated, but felt herself rising to her feet, moving to stand a few feet in front of him.

"Say that again. This time while looking me in the eyes." Sawyer's hand went to her hair, unconsciously twining a curl around her finger.

"I'm s—sorry. I never meant for anyone to be h—h—hurt." It was hard to meet his eyes with a guilty conscience berating her.

"That's better." Kaden's eyes studied her before he bent down to pick up the wet towel. Going into the bathroom, she saw him tossing it into the dirty clothes bin. He then leaned against the doorway.

"Tomorrow, we have one more concert before we take a week's break at R.J.'s house. The security team is spending their resources trying to keep you contained, and are failing on keeping the fans and press out. It's going to stop now, Sawyer. We are going to come to an agreement that's going to keep everyone safe."

"What do you mean? You're going to let me go?" Hope lightened the dread in her chest.

"No." Kaden's voice softened, but not by much. "What I mean is, do we both agree that five thousand isn't a drop in the bucket to what you actually need for you and your friend to disappear?"

She didn't want to admit it, but he was right. Five thousand would maybe keep them hidden a couple of months if they were frugal and she wasn't confident that with that amount of money they wouldn't be found.

"Y—yes."

"Then to secure your cooperation, I'm willing to give you three hundred thousand dollars for three months of your time."

Sawyer's mouth dropped open; she didn't know what to say.

"That should give us enough time to figure out what to do to fix the situation." Kaden wasn't going to let her go regardless of her answer; however, she was fully aware that they needed a large sum of money if they were going to be safe from Redman.

"I can't leave Vida without making sure she's safe."

"Vida is safe. Alec has checked it out, and she went to a man named King for protection."

Kaden was going to have to give her some more information if she was going to quit trying to escape.

"K—King?" Surprised, Sawyer didn't know what to think. King was certainly strong enough to keep Vida protected. He was also undoubtedly more capable than the police. He operated on his own ethical standards. Neither Vida nor she knew King very well, but King had never tried to harm them. In fact, from what she had found out after her mother's death, he had been keeping an eye on them for a very long time.

"Do you know him?"

"Not very well. He would come by the apartment building Vida and I lived in when we were kids. I never knew who he visited or why he was there. Mom told me one time that he controlled Queen City. It was only when I got older that I realized how."

"Is your friend safe with him?"

King ran several strip clubs, dealt in prostitution and drugs. Sawyer wanted to say no, but a memory from her childhood had her changing her opinion.

"Yes. I don't know why, but he feels he owes us a favor."

Kaden's gaze sharpened on her. Sawyer felt it without understanding his interest in King.

"I—I really don't know why. When we were little, Vida and another friend of mine and me were playing. To make a long story short, some boys in our neighborhood started messing with us and threw a doll out into the road. Callie ran out after it and Vida chased after her. I managed to save both from being hit by a car. King told me afterward that he owed me. Not long afterward, he put a protection order out in the neighborhood that we weren't to be touched."

"Why did he owe you? For saving Callie or Vida? Was he related to either of them?"

"N—no, C—Callie didn't even know who he was, while Vida was like me; we knew who he was because our mothers warned us how dangerous he could be."

"Could Vida be connected to King? Maybe that's why she went to him for help?"

"I doubt it. She would have told me."

"Okay. So do you believe that Vida will be safe with King?"

"Yes." She was reluctant to admit it, yet it was the truth.

"So will you stop your escape attempts now that you know Vida is safe?"

Unable to bear the scrutiny in his eyes, she turned away to sit on the side of the bed. It was a relief to know that Vida was safe.

"I can't forget about those women kidnapped for the next three months." How could he expect her to feel nothing for the women she had lain in a dark room with, hearing their cries for help every night?

She heard Kaden's frustrated sigh before his words had her staring back at him in confusion. "Alec is taking care of it, Sawyer. That's all I can tell you for now. You have to trust me. Did I let Rick take you and the other women? Haven't I kept you safe? The other women who Rick sent to the hotel are safe and can't be touched, either."

Sawyer had no reason to trust him. He had held her locked up for several weeks. So how could she possibly depend on him? Yet she did. He hadn't hurt her. In fact, his band and he had been hurt because of her. They were taking a chance to help her and possibly destroying their career that provided them with a very lucrative income. Surely they wouldn't jeopardize their livelihood unless they thought they were doing the right thing.

This time it was Sawyer who sighed. She was out of options; she really didn't have a choice in the matter. Either she could stay their hostage for the next three months or be a paid hostage with enough money to provide Vida and her the opportunity to start over without Redman finding them.

"Okay." Sawyer had no other choice; she gave in to his blackmail.

"We have a deal?"

"We have a deal." Sawyer felt as if she had just sold a part of herself she would never get back.

Chapter Eight

Sawyer stood backstage watching Mouth2Mouth perform on the monitor; they were mesmerizing. She had learned the hard way that watching them from a few feet away was overwhelming. She could understand the crowd's response of shouts and trying to get closer to the stage, which the security had to keep heavily guarded in order to push them back.

Kaden was singing with Alyce on the stage. They were dancing in a way that looked more like humping to Sawyer, and the crowd was going nuts. Alyce's ass was grinding back on Kaden's dick as his arms circled her waist with his hands pressed flat on her stomach, pulling her back to him. How they could concentrate on the words to the song she didn't know. The sexual tension was apparent between the two and everyone around them felt it. D-mon and Sin's eyes were surveying the crowd and Sawyer wondered who they would pick for a quickie before the bus left the arena.

The encore over, the lights dimmed and the band exited the stage to applause that sounded throughout the whole arena.

"Let's go," Alec said as they passed at the same time that Sawyer spotted D-mon giving a motion of his hand toward a pretty woman still trying to get near the stage, letting the security guard know who he'd chosen.

Turning, she followed the band and Alec as they returned to the VIP room, which quickly filled with press and fans who were allowed admittance. Sawyer found an empty chair, making herself comfortable for the next hour. Kaden had told her that they would be staying on the bus tonight as they drove to R.J.'s home.

They would stay there for the week before resuming the concert tour. It had never felt less like spring to her. She hoped Vida was having a better time than she was, but doubted it, how much fun could it be watching women strip?

She watched the band take photos and sign autographs as Alyce once again managed to stick by Kaden, making sure they were photographed together each time. The woman couldn't have made it more obvious that she was attracted to Kaden, and he flirted back, causing the sexual tension to become increasingly evident with each concert. It was only a matter of time before they acted on it, if they hadn't already done so. Sometimes, to alleviate the boredom, someone would ride on Alyce's bus. Kaden had disappeared twice for a few hours before coming back.

Sawyer looked away when she saw Alyce stand on her toes to brush her mouth against his just as another picture was taken.

She noticed all the men in the room were agitated tonight. D-mon and Sin, both heavy drinkers, were really hitting the liquor tonight. Without a doubt, both men were going to have serious hangovers in the morning. The woman who had been picked from the audience was wedged between the two men on the couch, clearly overwhelmed by the attention she was receiving from them both.

D-mon stood to his feet, taking the woman's hand

before leading her into the bathroom off the VIP room. The surprising part was when Sin got to his feet to follow behind them, and Sawyer saw all three enter the bathroom.

She took a drink of water as she tore her gaze away from the closed door.

"You doing okay?" Ax asked, sitting down on the arm of her chair.

"Yes, you did great tonight, Ax." She smiled at the band member who she felt the most relaxed with as he sprawled his long legs out in front of him.

"I thought most bands left after the concert?" Sawyer asked the question that had been on her mind since the first concert.

"Most do, but I suppose we stay because we started out playing in local bars and would hang out afterward, and due to the fact that we're touring so heavily right now, it gives us a break from the bus." His eyes smiled into hers, making her aware he had known what had caught her attention before he had sat down. "Besides, D-mon and Sin like to unwind after a show, so unless we stay at a hotel, they do their socializing before we get back on the bus."

Sawyer actually understood. While the bus was opulently furnished, and the most had been made of the space, it was still confining, especially with so many people on board.

"It's going to be nice to take a break and sleep in an actual bed for a week," Ax confided.

"You're not missing your family?"

"My parents are both in Australia, so I would spend more time traveling, which I'm sick of right now."

The bathroom door opened and the woman came out, flushed, and with her hair a mess, while both Sin and D-mon returned with a more relaxed air about them.

"I guess that means we can go," Ax said, starting to stand.

"Kaden and you don't meet and greet the locals?"

Sawyer felt herself turning red when he hesitated, staring down at her.

"No, we don't do quickies," he said with a wicked grin before leaving.

Just then, Alec motioned to her and she rose to her feet. *I'm really beginning to feel like a lapdog*, she thought resentfully.

The crowd outside the arena had thinned, so it wasn't an ordeal to pass through the door to get back on the bus. Sawyer went directly back to her room, tired tonight. They had taken an extra encore tonight, plus hung out a couple of hours. She wanted to shower and climb into bed.

Unfortunately, Kaden was a few steps behind her, his hand preventing her from shutting the door.

"I need to take a shower," Kaden said, coming into the room. Sawyer took a step back, letting him enter.

He went to the closet, gathered his clothes and went into the bathroom without a backward glance. Sawyer stuck her tongue out at the door then, feeling childish at her response, she flipped on the television.

She had watched more television the last few weeks than she had in years. If she didn't find something to occupy her mind soon, she was going to scream. The bus jarred slightly then quit. The bathroom door opened and Kaden came out, making Sawyer get to her feet to use the restroom, using the opportunity to escape his presence while he finished dressing. At that moment, the bus gave a loud pop and swerved.

Sawyer lost her balance, putting her hands out to stop herself from falling at the same time that Kaden reached out, managing to grab her just as the bus swerved again, sending them both to the floor. Sawyer landed heavily on top of Kaden, fearing they were about to crash, and then was relieved when the bus came to a stop.

"What happened?" Sawyer gasped, staring down into Kaden's eyes.

"I'd say we have a flat," Kaden answered, staring up at

her.

Sawyer started to get to her feet, aware of his large body lying underneath hers; however, a hand on the back of her neck stopped her.

"What's your hurry?" Kaden gave her what she was sure was a smile that landed him in many women's beds.

"I—is this you flirting with me?"

His hand on the back of her neck started caressing the sensitive skin.

"And if I am?" Again came the insincere smile meant to turn her bones to water.

"T—then I'd say don't waste your time." Sawyer clamored to her feet, making sure her elbow jabbed into his ribs.

Kaden winced as he got to his own feet. "Why?"

Sawyer's mouth dropped open, and then she closed it with a snap. "I don't know, maybe because you wouldn't let me leave when I wanted to. It's called kidnapping."

"We've worked that all out." She couldn't believe the arrogant man thought that she would just forget that he hadn't let her go.

"This conversation is over. It just shows how big an ass you are." Sawyer turned to go into the bathroom, giving him a disgusted look.

The anger that came over his face had Sawyer realizing a man like Kaden could take no for an answer, but challenging him was a different matter.

He moved to block her path. "Exactly what should I have done, Sawyer? Let you call the police so those other women Redman has could disappear? Or open the door and let you leave and give Redman the opportunity to have you before you managed to take two steps out the hotel door?" His lean body came nearer to hers, forcing her to move backwards until she came up against the edge of the bed. Sawyer forced herself to stay still.

"Y—you could have given me the c—choice."

"You weren't making good decisions. You're still not."

"How am I not making good decisions, Kaden?" Sawyer got right back in his face. "Because I don't let you fuck me like those airheads begging for dick back at the arena? If you needed to get laid, you should have taken a turn with D-mon and Sin or taken Alyce up on what she's been throwing at you."

"Why should I stand in line or have what I've already had, when I have you staring at me all the time. If you want to find out what you've been imagining, then all you have to do is ask."

Sawyer's hand flew out, striking him across his face. Her anger and embarrassment making her react without thinking.

"You know what really makes me angry?" Kaden's face turned stone cold. "When women want to hit men and not expect the same." Sawyer's face paled as he jerked her to him; her breasts pressed flat against his chest. "And I really don't like it when they do it because they don't like that I'm telling them the truth and don't want to fucking admit it."

"I—I don't want you," Sawyer denied.

"Prove it."

Sawyer wanted to smack him again, but decided not to press her luck. "Fuck off." She moved to go around him, and this time, he didn't move to block her path.

"Chicken." It wasn't a question; it was a statement.

Sawyer swung angrily back around to face him. "I'm not afraid of you, Kaden."

"I don't doubt you, by the way you just smacked me. What I was referring to was to you wanting to fuck me." His attitude was bringing out the ginger in her.

"Read my lips, you arrogant ass, I do not want you."

"Prove it." Sawyer put her hands in her jeans pockets, not sure she could restrain herself from strangling the man. "It's okay, Sawyer. A lot of women have a problem resisting me."

Before she could stop herself, she took a step forward,

pressing herself against him, her arms going around his neck. Dragging his head down to hers, she plastered her lips to his. The kiss was brief and passionless as his lips remained unresponsive and closed.

Sawyer didn't have a lot of experience with different men, but she had considered herself fairly good at kissing. Now she began to doubt herself as her tongue teased the seam of his lips and he still didn't let her deepen the kiss. Kaden lifted his mouth from her exploring lips, moving away.

"You've proven your point. I'll let you get your shower now. See you in the morning."

Confused, Sawyer stared at him, biting her lip. "I—I don't understand." She wanted to take back her words as soon as she spoke, but Kaden paused before walking back to her.

"Did you want me to respond or did you just want to prove that you could make me want you while you held yourself back?" Both, Sawyer admitted frankly to herself. "If you want me to respond, you have to kiss me the way I like to kiss. You didn't. It was an okay kiss, nothing special."

"W—what did I do wrong?" She frowned at him.

She had kissed him like she had the few other men she had kissed. She didn't think she was as bad at it as he seemed to think she was.

Kaden moved closer to her, keeping his arms by his side.

"You want my mouth, you ask for it." Sawyer licked her lips, wanting to disappear into the bathroom, but it had become a matter of pride with her. Despite all the warnings buzzing through her mind, she had never backed down from anyone yet.

Feeling ridiculous, she forged ahead. "Can I kiss you?" Sawyer asked, feeling stupid.

"*May* I kiss you," Kaden repeated the phrase the way he wanted her to express it.

Sure now that she was gradually swimming out of her depth, she repeated his words. "May I kiss you?"

"Yes."

This time Sawyer raised herself up to reach his mouth with hers. It was different from the moment their lips met. His mouth was warm and responsive, giving her what she had expected the first time she had kissed him. Her tongue timidly traced his lips, entering the warm recesses of his mouth when he opened his, allowing her entrance. He tasted like peppermint. The warmth making her want to draw closer to him.

She leaned into him, giving him more of her weight. Her nipples under her thin sweater and bra hardened as she felt his chest against hers. Her hands swept across his chest, feeling the firm flesh covered with tats.

He took his mouth away, drawing a reluctant whimper from her.

"Did I give you permission to touch me?" She saw from his clear gaze that he hadn't been as affected as she was by their kiss.

"N—no," she whispered.

"I expect you to ask, Sawyer."

She was definitely certain she was out of her depth, but she pressed on, not wanting to stop kissing him.

"Can—" At his frown, she stopped. "May I touch you?"

"Yes." Sawyer leaned back into him at the same time she reached up to take his mouth again. This time he met her halfway, taking control of the kiss, opening her mouth to his exploration. Her body melted against his, her arms hesitantly sliding around his neck as his hand curled around her hips, pulling her even closer.

The chemistry between them could easily get out of control if she wasn't careful, and she was about to call a halt, when again he pulled away from her.

"They should be done getting the tire fixed by now. I need to check and make sure everything is okay."

Sawyer stood still, her breathing uneven, as she lowered her arms to her sides.

"Goodnight, Sawyer." He then left without waiting for her reply.

Sawyer stood, staring at the closed door, until she felt the bus start moving again. She then went into the bathroom and took off her clothes before stepping into the shower.

Ignoring the warning in her head had been the biggest mistake of her life; however, her fighting instincts had her refusing to back down from his challenge. She had to be smart and bide her time until he gave her the money he'd promised. Then Vida and she could disappear to live the life they had always dreamed. All she had to do was keep her distance from Kaden for the next three months. Then, she would be free.

Sawyer knew it was going to be easier said than done.

Chapter Nine

Sawyer sat at the kitchenette table drinking a cup of coffee, when the bus driver told them they were an hour away from R.J.'s house. She was looking forward to getting off the bus for a few days. She had been getting sick to her stomach from the motion of the bus when she had first started out with the band. Alec had given her a bottle of medicine—which she would dab a small amount behind her ear every morning— and it had made the constant motion of the bus more bearable; however, the confining space, with so much male testosterone was beginning to wear on her nerves. That, combined with the food, was making her want to throw a screaming fit. The only thing holding her back was the embarrassment of making a fool of herself.

Ax slid into the seat across from her. "Getting stir crazy?"

"I don't know if I could take one more day on this bus," Sawyer confessed.

"It gets to us all. That's why we have to take intermittent breaks. Without them, arguments start and it affects the performances."

"I can understand that. I feel like punching something myself."

"Don't do well being confined, huh?"

Sawyer shook her head. "No, it reminds me too much of my childhood." She looked outside the window at the passing scenery. Unaware the others had stopped playing cards and were listening to her conversation with Ax. She had always kept to herself, but thinking about her childhood had made her melancholy, lowering her guard.

"Your parents kept you confined on a bus?" Ax asked teasingly.

"No, our apartment was smaller than this and definitely not as well decorated." Sawyer's lips tightened as her memories played in her mind. Her hand went to her hair, twisting a lock of her reddish gold hair around her finger over and over again.

"A—after my father was killed in a car accident, my mother became over-protective. She babysat other children to earn money, so I stayed home with her until kindergarten. The only friends I had were the other children she babysat. We thought we were sisters. We didn't understand until we were four or five that we weren't related.

"Because we didn't live in the best neighborhood, she was afraid to let us go outside to play. As we grew older and went to school, we would always sneak and play for a few minutes before we went inside, because once we were inside, she wouldn't let us back out. Vida, Callie and I learned to make the most of that time. We would drive everyone in the neighborhood and apartment building crazy." Sawyer paused, blinking back tears. She missed those times so badly. Sometimes she looked back and thought that those moments with Vida and Callie were the best times in her life, and then her mother's stern face had her thinking the opposite.

"It sounds like you were all close."

Sawyer's smile was sadly reminiscent.

"We were. We were so different. Vida is a brunette, Callie had black hair, and me with my red hair always made it easy to identify the culprit of our crimes. They would, of course, tell our mothers. My mother would make me stay in for several days. Vida's mom was laid back so she never got into too much trouble."

"How about Callie? Was her mom like yours or Vida's?" Ax asked softly, as if he knew she was lost in the past.

"Neither. Brenda never let Callie out much. She never went to Kindergarten. Brenda kept telling social services she was too sick." Unconsciously, Sawyer's hand went back to a red curl, tugging and pulling at the tendril over and over. "When she would get in trouble, Brenda would beat her. She blacked her eye one time, and everyone in the apartment building knew it. Not one adult tried to stop her though."

"Did she get in trouble a lot?"

"Oh, yes, but none of it was her fault. After Brenda blacked her eye, no one would help, but they made sure no one told on her anymore." Sawyer took a shuddering breath. "We made plans to run away together when we got older. We borrowed books from the library and looked at all the places we dreamed of going." A lone tear streaked her cheek. "I wanted to go to Disneyland while Vida wanted to live on a farm."

"Where did Callie want to go?" Ax's soft question brought a smile to her lips.

"She wanted to go to Alaska. I had told her about the Northern Lights and she wanted to see them. Vida and I researched it for hours for her. Did you know that sometimes, if the conditions are right, they can be seen in Texas and even New Orleans?"

"No, I didn't know that."

"We knew that we didn't stand a chance of making it to Alaska, though it made her so happy when we told her that the lights could be seen from Texas. I'll never forget the day we told her. Her smile…" Sawyer's voice broke off.

"Have any of you gotten to go where you wanted?"

"Vida and I went to Disneyland last year. I know it sounds silly, but we had a good time. Then Vida spent a summer off from school working at a farmers' market. That's as close as she got."

"How about Callie?"

"No, she never got to see the Northern Lights."

"Vida's the one that's with King?" Ax questioned. Sawyer nodded her head.

"If Redman is after you and Vida for your connection to King, then isn't this Callie in danger also?"

Sawyer was dragged away from her memories by Kaden's voice. She turned toward him and saw everyone looking at her, realizing belatedly that they were unashamedly listening to her conversation with Ax.

"No one can touch that sweet girl ever again." Sawyer slid out of the booth. Her face was a mask hiding her emotions, though she was unaware of the tortured look in her eyes that couldn't be concealed. "She died in a fire when she was eight years old."

The silence in the room was deafening as she went into the bedroom to gather the few items of clothing R.J. had purchased for her.

"I'm sorry about your friend." Kaden's soft apology had her shoulders stiffening, but she didn't turn around. She had made a point of making sure she wasn't caught in the act of staring at him again.

"Thanks." Sawyer picked up the bag of clothing and toiletries, intending to go back out with the others.

"You've been avoiding me." Kaden's directness drew her gaze to him.

"It's hard to avoid someone on a bus this size," Sawyer said evasively.

"You manage to leave the room every time you see me."

"Kaden, I don't like playing games and obviously you

do. I think it's best we have as little contact as possible until I leave."

"I see, so you think this is a game?"

"I think you're an experienced player, Kaden," Sawyer countered.

"You know what I think, Sawyer? I think you're scared to death of what's going on between us, but you go right ahead and ignore it if you want to. I'll give you a warning, though; the next time you want me to kiss you, I won't make you ask me. I'll make you beg."

Kaden turned, leaving her standing there, staring at him with apprehension growing in her chest.

* * *

Sawyer was one of the last off the bus. The waitress in her had been unable to leave the dirty dishes in the sink. When she finished, she stepped out of the bus, going inside to a room filled with the band members and several women still squealing at their arrival. She began to get angry, thinking R.J. was up to his old tricks when she heard the men calling the women by name.

Sin had an exotic woman hanging around his neck with a hand on her butt. D-mon was kissing a leggy blonde, and even Ax had a blonde gazing up at him adoringly while his arm circled her shoulder. R.J. had a brunette welcoming him home at the same time that Kaden and Alec were both talking to some of the security who she had seen during the concerts. There were three other women lounging around with wine glasses in their hand, dressed in designer jeans and tees. Those women, Sawyer guessed, were for Kaden to take his pick. These women weren't sex slaves to anyone unless they were the ones holding someone captive. Their curious stares raised the hair on her arms as she understood the cat-like speculation they contained.

Alec excused himself, coming toward her. "Let me show you to your room. Then you can come down to dinner. R.J. hired a cook. It's going to be good to have home cooking again."

Sawyer silently agreed. The only food supply they'd kept on the bus was premade meals, sandwiches and snacks. When the band was really hungry, they would do take out or buffet. Both of which Sawyer was sick of.

Alec opened the door to a bedroom of pale lavender and gold, which was decorated with expensive furnishings that had her wincing at how out of place she was.

"Kaden called ahead and asked R.J.'s assistant to pick up some more clothes for you. I believe she put them away for you. I'll see you in a few minutes."

Sawyer stood uncertainly in the room, not sure what to do next. She went to the closet, opening the door to find a walk-in closet with a vast array of clothes still with the tags on.

Her hand touched one of the silky tops, rubbing the soft material between her fingertips. She could never afford clothes like these. A shiny silver dress caught her eye. It was sexy hanging on the hanger, and she doubted she would ever have the courage to wear such an expensive dress.

Going back out into the bedroom, she searched the drawers, finding more casual clothes. Unable to bring herself to put on the new, stiff jeans she found, she went to her bag, pulling out her more comfortable jeans that she was sure R.J. had hastily purchased at a discount store. Her remaining two tops were dirty, so she had to cave and pick one of the delicate tops that had been purchased for her.

She soaked for thirty minutes in the big tub, enjoying the luxury of the bath's shampoo and soaps she found, before forcing herself to get out of the tub when she began to grow sleepy. She dried off and dressed, dreading going back downstairs.

She had never been able to mix comfortably with strangers, and the house filled with women made her feel uncomfortable. She should be excited having other women to talk to, but somehow, she didn't think any of the women were in the search for a new friend.

Her empty stomach had her leaving the bedroom, returning downstairs to find Ax and one woman sitting at the table as well as Kaden and his harem, she thought snarkily. R.J., his wife—she discovered was named Briana—and Alec were also sitting at the dining table. "Have a seat. My name is Briana. I'm married to R.J. I'll ask the housekeeper to bring an extra plate for you." She gave a genuine smile as she started to rise from the table.

"Don't bother. I can get it for myself," Sawyer said, going into the kitchen before Briana could protest. She stopped short at the sight that met her eyes.

A pretty young woman was trying desperately to put out a small fire on the stove. Without thought, Sawyer hurriedly rushed over, taking a lid off another pot to smother the flame.

"Thanks. I don't know what I was going to do if you hadn't come in when you had."

"Call the fire truck?" Sawyer grinned, returning the woman's friendly smile.

"I would have let the house burn down before that happened. I'm trying to land a permanent job; I can't call a fire truck. It would cause too much attention."

"And a blazing fire wouldn't?" Sawyer laughed at the woman's convoluted thinking.

"I wouldn't have let it get that far. I would have thrown my own body over it first."

Sawyer whistled in admiration. "You must want this housekeeping job bad."

Now it was the other woman's turn to laugh. "No, I'm afraid I'm at a total loss as a housekeeper, but I would make a great personal assistant. The housekeeper came down with the stomach flu. I'm interning for a job as R.J.'s personal assistant, so guess who gets to fill in for her?"

Her ineptitude explained, Sawyer helped her clean the mess on the stove, removing the pan that had caused the fire to the sink. Going back to the stove, she checked on the food still cooking. To call it a disaster was being polite.

Sawyer rolled her sleeves up and tried to save the meal as best she could, giving the woman directions as she cooked the meal. When Ax stuck his head in the door later, seeing Sawyer helping, he gave a wink then left them to fill the plates.

"You take those two, I'll take these." Sawyer lifted the two plates on the counter, leaving three other ones. "I'll come back and get those," Sawyer said, going through the swinging door.

Sawyer sat one of her plates down in front of R.J. and the other in front of Briana. The other two plates were sat in front of Ax and his companion. Sawyer started to go back to help with the remaining plates.

"Sit down, Sawyer." Kaden's firm voice brought her to a standstill.

"I—I won't be a second."

"Sit down." He stood up, pulling a chair out for her.

"Ms. Jordan can handle the rest. Have a seat, Sawyer," R.J. broke in the staring contest between her and Kaden.

She looked at the young woman, noticing her worried frown and gave in, taking a seat at the table.

She looked across the table to see Ax trying to hide his amusement as he ate his food, at the same time that a plate was slid in front of her. Giving into her own hunger, she began eating.

The food was good. The potatoes were creamy and so was the undercooked meat she had managed to save while making a quick pan of gravy. The asparagus she had roasted melted in her mouth. The silence at the table was due to the fact that everyone was enjoying the food as much as her.

"Can I get anyone anything else?" the sweet voice of R.J.'s assistant had her smiling as the young woman nervously waited for everyone's reaction.

"No, thank you, Ms. Jordan. That was delicious. We've missed having a good meal lately and that made up for it.

I'm looking forward to breakfast," R.J. said as an afterthought.

Sawyer barely hid her laughter at the look of panic crossing her face before she could hide it. Sawyer decided to set her alarm so that she could rise early enough to help her.

The woman disappeared back into the kitchen as they rose from the table. Sawyer was still angry at Kaden for ordering her around, but he ignored her as he went into the other room with two of the other women guests. Sawyer had no intention of watching the women flirt with him for the rest of the night, instead deciding to go to bed early.

She caught Briana before she went into the formal living room.

"I'm going to go to bed."

"It's pretty early," Briana protested half-heartedly. Sawyer felt that the woman wasn't anxious for her company, either. R.J. must have told her why she was with the band, or perhaps she simply stuck out like a sore thumb compared to the other women.

Sawyer went up the steps to the bedroom, closing the door behind her. She went to the drawers and pulled out one of the new nightgowns that had been purchased for her. Getting changed, she enjoyed the feel of the silky material sliding over her skin. Her nipples tightened against the material. Sawyer ran her hand through her hair as she went to her bag, pulling out her brush before passing it through her long hair. Brushing her hair had always soothed her.

As she continued to brush, she walked barefoot across the carpeted floor, going to the window and pulling the curtain open. She stared out into the night, seeing a large pool lit up. R.J. and the band must have gone outside to enjoy the fresh air. The pool area was well lit, so Sawyer had no difficulty making out who sat around the pool.

Kaden was sitting on one of the lounge chairs with a

pretty woman sitting next to him, while her hand was casually rubbing his thigh.

"I wonder if she asked his permission?" she said into the silence of the bedroom.

Almost as if he could hear her voice, his eyes lifted to the window she was standing at. Sawyer froze in place as his gaze took in the gown she was wearing, her hair framing her face. The hand holding the brush dropped to her side, realizing belatedly it was the movement of her brushing her hair that had drawn his attention to her window.

She dropped the curtain, taking a shaky step back. Setting the brush down on the nightstand, she turned out the light before climbing into bed. It was getting harder and harder to ignore the escalating tension between her and Kaden. She had been around several good-looking men the last few years as a waitress, but had never experienced the desire to get to know any of them. It was a constant battle, however, to stay away from Kaden. The only thing saving her was her instinctive dislike of him. God help her if she ever discovered he was a nice guy under that sexy body.

Chapter Ten

Sawyer was busy in the kitchen when R.J.'s assistant came in.

"You shouldn't be in here. Mr. Cross wasn't happy that you helped out last night. R.J. had a talk with me after dinner." She went to the counter to pour herself a cup of coffee, taking a piece of stuffed cinnamon toast. Sawyer watched her in amusement, noticing R.J.'s talk didn't stop the woman from taking advantage of the available food.

"Ms. Jordan." Sawyer paused. "What's your first name? I can't keep calling you Ms. Jordan."

"Just call me Jordan." Her twinkling eyes laughed at Sawyer. "He doesn't want us getting friendly. That's not in my job description," she mocked R.J.'s snobby attitude.

Sawyer rolled her eyes. If the young woman knew just to what depths R.J. would sink to keep the band happy, his professional façade would be exposed.

"I can live with calling you Jordan." Sawyer went to pour herself a cup of coffee before taking a seat at the kitchen table.

They sat and talked for several minutes, and Sawyer discovered she liked the woman. She was around Vida's age. She also was friendly, bubbly and wanted to prove to R.J. that she could handle the job as his assistant.

Kaden came into the kitchen as they finished their coffee. When he went to pour himself a cup, Sawyer escaped without a word, trying not to wonder if he had spent the night with the woman she had seen him with the previous night. Stir crazy and not wanting to return to her room, she went out the front door. It was pretty outside. Wanting to stretch her legs, she wandered around the side of the house to the pool area. Bored, she sank down onto one of the lounge chairs, trying to think of something to keep herself occupied.

"Are you going to run off if I take a seat?" Kaden stood next to her chair, waiting for her answer.

"N —no, and I—I wasn't running. I was finished," Sawyer clarified.

Expecting him to sit down in the lounger next to her, he instead sat down beside her hip, facing the house. He had put on a pair of sunglasses; the dark lenses stared down at her, giving him a ruthless appearance.

"How did you get to the pool?"

Confused by his question, she frowned up at him. "I walked?"

"I know that," he said impatiently, "but I was in the kitchen, and I could see the only other entrance to the pool and you didn't come out that way."

"I went out the front door. I wanted to take a walk. I walked beside the house and it led back here," she explained. She couldn't understand why he looked angry. She hadn't tried to leave; she had just wanted out of the house for a few minutes.

Sawyer looked up at him cautiously, wishing she had just gotten up and gone back indoors to the safety of Jordan's company.

"Don't go back out front again unless me or one of the other men are with you. Alec let some of the men go home while we're on break; there's only a skeleton staff for security."

Again, through no fault of her own, she was confined. She had no more freedom here than she'd had on the bus.

"Why are you looking so unhappy? The other women seem happy enough to be here."

"I'm bored. I'm sorry if I don't find hanging out with your band entertaining," Sawyer snapped.

"What did you do before you were kidnapped?"

"I worked; I was a waitress. I shared a small apartment with Vida."

"To me that sounds boring."

It was. Vida was constantly studying, and with no other friends, she had often found herself at a loose end.

"What did you do to keep yourself occupied?" Kaden questioned her perceptively.

"I cooked. Vida constantly studied, so I cooked when I became bored. I would take what I made to the homeless shelter down the street." Sawyer didn't realize she had let it slip that she didn't live in one of the safest areas of Queens City.

"I see. You didn't want to go to college with your friend?"

Sawyer shook her head regretfully. "I hated school. I was never good at it and was happy to get out of high school. I didn't want to tie myself down to four more years of misery."

"You're planning on being a waitress for the rest of your life?"

"No, smartass, I don't. When Vida graduates this semester, we had plans to travel. I was going to learn about different cuisines. I planned on going to cooking school once we decided where we were going to settle down."

"How were you planning on supporting yourself when you went to school?" Kaden asked her.

"I took care of all the bills while Vida earned her degree. She was going to take care of expenses when I went to school. We had it all planned out." Sawyer's lips trembled as she thought of the many nights they had sat planning their future together.

"What if one of you met someone and decided to go your own way?"

"We wouldn't do that to each other. We both want to travel too much."

"You're getting to travel now," he reasoned.

"It isn't the same. No one lets me cook, and when I do, Jordan gets in trouble." Not so subtly she was letting him know she hadn't appreciated his interference last night.

"Ms. Jordan didn't get in trouble for your helping to cook. The guy's were too starved for that. What I don't want to see again is you serving anyone."

Sawyer frowned up at him. "It's what I do. I enjoy it. It's nothing to be embarrassed about."

"So it's just my orders you don't want to take?"

She didn't think his twist on her words was funny.

"Let me up." Sawyer tried to get up from the lounge chair, but Kaden—who had continued sitting by her hip—put his hand beside her opposite hip to pin her to the lounger without touching her, effectively preventing her escaping back into the house.

"Why is it that you're always running away from me when you don't have any trouble talking to Ax, D-mon or Sin?"

As his hand reached out, his thumb brushing her cheekbone, she jerked her face away from his touch.

"Did I give you permission to touch me?" This time it was Sawyer throwing his words back in his face.

Kaden gave a low, seductive laugh. "Did that make you angry, Sawyer? I didn't mean to make you angry. Which do you appreciate more: something easily given, or something you have to ask for, something you crave?"

"I didn't notice that woman sitting next to you last night asking to touch you."

He shrugged nonchalantly. "Did you see me touch her back?"

Sawyer had to admit to herself that she hadn't seen him touch the woman back.

"Do you want to know if I fucked her last night, Sawyer?" Kaden asked, leaning down to whisper his question in her ear.

Sawyer trembled under his seductive spell. She had never been so intensely pursued by a man before. She'd had several that had flirted with her—even Rick when he had been luring her into his sick web of lies had made her feel wanted—but she had always been aware that he would forget about her five minutes after leaving the restaurant. She had eventually agreed to go out with him because he had discovered her desire to eat at one of the finer restaurants in town whose chef had recently won a prestigious cooking award.

"N—no, I don't, Kaden. I—I don't care who you fuck," Sawyer lied to both of them.

"I didn't. I believe Alana ended up in Sin's bed after he finished with Megan."

"How benevolent of him to share himself around," Sawyer said, disgusted.

"I believe that's what he thinks. I, on the other hand, have learned that quality is much more exciting than quantity, so I spent my night taking cold showers and jerking off, thinking about you."

Sawyer's eyes flew to his, seeing that he wasn't joking. "S—stop it, K—Kaden."

"Stop what, Sawyer? I haven't laid a hand on you and I won't until you beg. I just want to let you know, tonight when you're in your thin gown with those nipples hard, that all you have to do is come next door to my room, and I'll give you what you're craving. I'll sink my dick in your tight little pussy and ride you all night long. All you have to do is ask me nicely."

Sawyer felt the heat build in the area he was mentioning. She almost stretched out underneath him then and there. The only thing holding her back was her anger at the way he had refused to let her contact the police and an instinct inside her that was screaming that he wanted her total capitulation, which she couldn't give.

"I—I will never beg for you, Kaden, but if you get bored waiting for me, why don't you hold your breath while you're waiting."

"That remark going to cost you a punishment when you give in, Sawyer." Kaden stood up. "I have some work to do, so if you're bored, go and have fun in the kitchen if you want, but remember what I said, Sawyer. I better not catch you handing anyone a glass of water if they're dying of thirst." His hard gaze had her nipples tightening. She was so angry at her body's betraying response.

"Go fuck y—yourself." His eyes dropped to her nipples before he gave a mysterious smile.

"Why is it you only stutter when you get nervous?" He didn't give her time to answer, walking away from the lounge chair and leaving her a hot mess.

She ran an anxious hand through her hair, trying to gather control of her body now that he had gone. One thing was for sure, her trying to stay out of his way had been an epic fail. She was going to have to come up with a better battle plan or she was going to be in trouble trying to resist a man who had enough sex appeal that a freaking nun would throw her panties at him, and Sawyer sure as hell was not a nun.

Being given free rein of the kitchen allowed Sawyer a sense of control that she hadn't experienced since her kidnapping. Jordan helped out by making a run to the grocery store with her list. While she was gone, Sawyer threw together a light lunch that Jordan could serve them when she returned.

Going upstairs, she showered and changed before going back downstairs to help Jordan put away the groceries.

At lunchtime, she forced herself to leave Jordan to go to the dining room, taking a seat at the table. It went against her personality to sit and let Jordan do all the work, but not wanting to be banned from the kitchen, she gave in to Kaden's demand.

After lunch, the women decided to go into town for an impromptu shopping trip.

They didn't even ask if she wanted to go, which she was thankful for.

"Let me change my shoes." Mila, D-mon's girlfriend, moved away, throwing the women at the table a warning glance before leaving the table. If the woman wasn't such a bitch, Sawyer would have told her D-mon was a horndog, but since she was one, Sawyer felt no compunction in not giving her a heads up.

"You don't want to go? I thought you'd jump at the opportunity to get out of the house," Kaden said as she rose to leave the table.

"No, thanks. I'll give it a pass."

Sawyer didn't try to explain. She had always found it difficult to make friends with women. These women here didn't want to be friends; they wanted what time they could get with the band, without an outsider trying to get inside their little group. Sawyer really couldn't blame them; they had to fight against the fans' attention all the time. Why would they want to during the band's alone time? She might not like the other women, but she could understand them.

Sawyer went upstairs to her room, planning on taking a nap. Hearing voices, she went to her side window and watched as the band and their guests climbed into two large cars. Kaden was wearing jeans, a t-shirt and sunglasses. The sun glinted on his hair. He was striking just standing there among the other men. Alana was standing next to him and they were talking before they slid into the car together.

Sawyer ignored the twist in her stomach before she went to the bed to lie down. Jordan had told her that she had been given the night off, that as they had made plans to eat out for the night. Alec had paid her a visit before he had left, warning her to stay in the house or by the pool.

Sawyer stretched out on the bed with nothing to look forward to other than another boring night. While the band partied in town, she had remained hiding in her room. Just once she wished she could find the courage to actually go out and be carefree, but growing up in the poorest section of Queen City had shown her the harsh reality of life. It was a lesson that her mother had constantly warned her of, without having to utter a single word.

Her mother had no other option but to move into the large low-income apartment building after her father's death. While his death had been unintentional, the apartment building had been filled with children being raised without fathers. There hadn't been a single man trapped by low income within those vicious walls, unless they had been living off one of the women, desperate for their company, or a son who was perpetuating their father's example.

She had watched Vida's mother suffer through each failed relationship, while Callie had never even known who her father was before being left in her mother's sadistic care, using men like used newspaper over and over again.

As she grew up, she had seen the consequences of foolishly loving someone. She had sworn that she would be smarter, wiser. She wouldn't fall in love and become destroyed. She wouldn't be held back with invisible chains, her heart held prisoner. She would be free.

Chapter Eleven

Sawyer woke up from her nap energized. Remembering the swimsuits in one of the drawers, she picked out a black one and changed into it before she could change her mind.

The security was at the front gate and Alec had gone into town with the band. Jordan had wanted to use her free time to catch up on some of R.J.'s work, so Sawyer had the house to herself.

She couldn't remember the last time she had gone swimming. Grabbing a towel, she went downstairs to the pool where she dropped the towel on one of the loungers before cautiously going in. She was pleasantly surprised when she found it was warm, which made her jump in. Coming up out of the water, she laughed, shaking her hair out of her face before she began swimming the length of the pool. Enjoying the silky feel of the water against her skin, she paused to catch her breath, leaning against the side of the pool.

Hearing a splash, she turned around, startled at the sound. As soon as she saw his shoulders, she knew it was Kaden. The other men were broader while Kaden was leaner.

He swam over to her. "I see you decided to quit being a hermit when everyone left." Kaden was able to stand and touch the bottom while the water was a few inches deeper for her because of her lack of height.

"I—I thought you left," Sawyer stated the obvious.

"I came back early," Kaden said with amusement glinting in his eyes.

Sawyer wasn't sure, but somehow she thought she had stepped in a trap. Not liking the feeling, she decided to go back inside.

"Not thinking of running away, are you?" he taunted.

Sawyer stiffened. "I'm not running away from you, Kaden. I just don't want to spend any time with you."

"Sawyer, you are definitely a woman not afraid of speaking her mind. " His eyes lowered to her scantily covered breasts. Placing one hand on the side of the pool next to her and another on the other side of her, he effectively trapped her between the pool and himself.

"You said you wouldn't touch me," Sawyer said in challenge.

"I haven't touched you yet, Sawyer," Kaden mocked her. "That doesn't mean I don't want to. I want to just as badly as you want to touch me."

Sawyer opened her mouth to give a remark, but he forestalled her. "Don't lie, Sawyer. I know you do."

"And how do you know that? Your vast experiences?"

"No, because of that hungry look in your eyes when you think I'm not paying attention. Don't be embarrassed." His eyes went to the flush rising on her cheeks. Sawyer would be damned if she wasn't able to control that reaction one day.

"I'm not embarrassed," Sawyer lied about her reaction without any qualms.

"Good. Because there is no reason to be. We're attracted to each other. That's nothing to be ashamed of. In fact, I think we should explore it further."

"I bet you do," Sawyer muttered under her breath.

Kaden laughed before staring intently into her eyes. "For example, I'd like to explore your breasts. I see your hard little nipples and I want to see what color they are. Are they pink, red or brown? How do they taste? That's what I need to know."

Sawyer stared back, the sexual tension between them escalating.

"Untie your top, Sawyer."

Sawyer shook her head, feeling like the water around her had just become deeper and she hadn't moved an inch.

"Now."

Sawyer's fingers moved to the tie behind her neck without knowing why; she only was aware that she didn't want to refuse him. Her fingers fumbled with the tie before it finally loosened.

"Take it off and hand it to me."

Her mind was screaming at what she was about to do, but for once, Sawyer ignored it. Her hand went behind her back to untie the last string. Removing her top, she placed it in Kaden's waiting hand. He laid it on the concrete beside her head where she could see it from the corner of her eye, a sure reminder that she was the one to give it up. Her eyes went to his face to see his eyes were staring at her breasts.

"There's only one question left, Sawyer. How do you taste? Do you want me to touch you? Suck that little bead into my mouth? Is that what you want, Sawyer?"

Sawyer didn't speak for several minutes before finally admitting the truth. "Y—Yes." Her voice was low and confused.

"What did you say?"

"Yes, Kaden." This time her voice was sure.

He had lied; he didn't make her beg. Instead, his head immediately lowered to her breasts, taking one of the nipples into his mouth, latching onto her tender nub with his teeth, while using the tip of his tongue to torment the captured nipple. The pressure caused her pussy to clench in need.

Her body responded to him quickly. She stiffened, arching her body, wanting him to take more of her breast into his mouth, but instead, he raised his head.

"Your nipple was pink. Now, it's a little, red berry," he said, giving it a final stroke of his tongue before lowering his head and capturing her other nipple, biting down on it slightly harder than the other. The small bite of pain had her clenching her thighs together under the water.

Again he raised his head. "Stop it, Sawyer."

Sawyer looked at him, understanding what he wanted her to stop.

"Spread your legs. If you need relief, I'm the only one allowed to do that for you." His firm jaw had her unclenching her thighs as his hands circled her waist, lifting her to sit on the edge of the pool.

Wildly, Sawyer looked around the empty backyard.

"Everyone went into town, and the guards at the front gate can't see through the trees."

Sawyer was still about to protest when his hands went to her hips again, untying the bottoms of her swimsuit before tugging them out from underneath her.

"Kaden…" Sawyer started to protest, yet before she could get out another word, Kaden's head went between her thighs, his tongue searching the fleshy lips of her pussy as his hand gripped her thighs, spreading her wider.

Sawyer was lost. She had never had a man go down on her and the unbelievable pleasure had her leaning back on her hands, raising her hips toward his exploring mouth.

When she had graduated high school and began waitressing, she had started seeing one of the managers at the restaurant she had worked for. She had never even told Vida.

He had explained to her it would make life difficult at work if it became known they were together, as he was one of the managers and her one of the staff.

For two months, he had weakened her resolve until she

had broken down and had sex with him. He had been more experienced than her, and had enjoyed her inexperience. Their time together was always rushed because of his long work schedule. He had never really taken the time to explore her body.

She had began to feel dirty after each encounter, as the only time they spent together was just long enough for him to reach his own climax before he was out the door. She hadn't been searching for love from him, but she had wanted to enjoy a sexual relationship like many women her age. Sadly, only one of them received all of the pleasure, and it sure as hell hadn't been her.

It was only when another waitress began working at the restaurant, and she noticed the attention he was paying her, that she came to the conclusion it was a challenge for him to get the new waitresses. When one of the older waitresses had confirmed her thoughts, Sawyer had been upset at herself because she hadn't chosen her first lover more wisely. Sawyer was a believer in live and learn.

She had learned to pick more wisely, and since then, had waited for someone who would want her enjoyment as much as his own. Kaden wanted to take her over until she had no control over her body, other than the pleasure he was giving her. Each time he touched her, it was about her pleasure taking, none for himself. It was actually escalating her own passion, giving her the control she had been missing since her kidnapping.

His hands slid her thighs over his shoulders as his tongue found her clit, licking the bud until his tongue exposed the sensitive nerves underneath. Her hips thrust toward him as he bit down on her when he felt her start to climax, stopping her from coming. He sought her opening and thrust his tongue inside her, fucking her with his tongue until she writhed on the hard concrete that was scratching her skin.

When the first helpless whimper parted her lips, his mouth left hers. His hands then took hers, levering her back into a sitting position. Taking her by the hips, he picked her up and brought her into the water once more, pinning her back against the side of the pool. The pleasure he had given her and the sudden movement of him bringing her back into the water momentarily disoriented her. His cock was already sliding inside the tight opening of her pussy before she had her senses back under control.

Sawyer gasped as he thrust into her. She felt him bury his length inside of her sheath. Her thighs went to his hips for leverage, about to jerk herself off his length, when Kaden's hands on her hips used her reaction to take a beaded nipple into his mouth, using her momentum to widen her thighs, sliding another thick inch inside of her.

"Kaden..." He was a tight fit inside of her. She had never had sex in water, and the tightness in her pussy was making it difficult for his cock to slide easily within her. Instead, she felt every movement his cock made as Kaden used his strength to lift her; then he let her weight help him thrust him through her tight passage.

Sawyer grabbed his shoulders as she tried to adjust herself on his cock, attempting to take him in. Kaden lifted his head, watching her breasts slap the water with their movements. The edge of pain had her nipples hardening.

"You are going to take me, Sawyer." Kaden's hard voice had her eyes rising to his as his mouth came down on hers. His tongue took control of hers as his cock took control of her pussy. Sawyer found a wildness rising inside of her that she didn't know how to control; tilting her hips forward to increase the pressure against her clit so she could climax and bring an end to the torture of need he was raising inside of her.

Kaden controlled her body easily, pressing her harder against the side of the pool. His cock effortlessly moved inside her, and had her thrusting back at him, forgetting she had been about to call a halt to his fucking her. The only thing in her mind was to reach the unbelievable orgasm he was driving her toward. She had given in to his demands easily and he was rewarding her with the pleasure she had searched for but hadn't found.

Kaden drove inside of her, clenching his hands on her ass to grind her down harder on his dick, making her gasp around his thrusting tongue. The simple action made her pussy clench, sending her over the edge into a climax that had her thrusting wildly against him.

Kaden groaned as he clasped her tighter against him before he groaned out his own release into her. "Fuck."

"Oh, my God." Sawyer tried to tear herself away from Kaden, horrified at her behavior.

"Stop it, Sawyer." Kaden held her struggling body still as his cock slid out of her. Sawyer winced at her recklessness. She hadn't even realized he hadn't been wearing a swimsuit in the pool.

"I—I can't believe we j—just—that I…" Sawyer's hand covered her mouth. "We didn't use any p—pro— otection. I'm no better than those women that Sin picks up." Sawyer felt herself getting hysterical.

"Sawyer, I have regular blood tests, and I haven't fucked anyone since my last blood test. So you won't catch anything from me." When she opened her mouth again, he cut her off. "You can't get pregnant, either. I had a vasectomy years ago. I have no desire for children in my life and I have no intention of paying child support for kids that aren't mine."

Sawyer's mouth dropped open.

"I don't like you at all," Sawyer said to herself and him. His hand went to her jaw, locking her eyes with his.

"You may not like me, Sawyer, but you are attracted to me and you sure as hell liked me fucking you. Don't even try to deny it when I can show you just how much."

Sawyer snapped her mouth shut not about to challenge him when they were both still naked.

"Let me go."

Kaden moved to her side and Sawyer turned to swim to the steps to get out of the pool. Kaden forestalled her, though; his arm going around her waist, lifting her back against him, his cock nestled against her ass.

"Run away, Sawyer. You're good at that." His hand glided between her thighs, brushing against her pussy.

Shuddering, Sawyer held herself still in his hold while his thumb brushed through her curls.

"I want this shaved. If you haven't taken care of it by the next time I fuck you, then I'll do it myself."

Sawyer forced herself to break free from his hold. "Go drown yourself, Kaden."

His mocking laughter followed her as she snatched up the towel she had brought outside and hastily wrapped it around herself before going in the house. She didn't run, but she wanted to. She was determined not to give him the satisfaction of seeing her fleeing, however.

Inside, she showered and changed into her jeans and t-shirt, ignoring the more expensive clothes. She sat down on the side of the bed and buried her face in her hands. The longer she stayed, the more she felt an imaginary noose tightening around her neck.

Her mother had strangled any amount of freedom Sawyer could even think of having until her murder. She'd loved her mother and still missed her, but had always felt their relationship was abnormal, with the way her mother would react every time she went out the door. It had become so bad with her demands and manipulations that Sawyer had resented her.

Sawyer had fought too long and too hard not to cave in to her mother's demands to let Kaden make her feel the same way.

She had to hold out against Kaden. Not only did he threaten to take away her hard won freedom, but he was also quickly guaranteeing that he would take her soul.

Chapter Twelve

Sawyer went back downstairs. Needing fresh air, she went out the front door, deciding to take a walk in the comfortable temperature. She walked down the driveway, enjoying the sunshine as the feeling of being confined began to evaporate.

Seeing the small guardhouse a few feet away, she belatedly remembered Kaden's warning and decided to turn back. The sound of a car screeching and pulling into the driveway had her freezing until she heard the distinctive sound of gunfire.

Sawyer began running, veering away from the driveway. She ran as fast as she could. There were not many trees, so she had no place to hide on R.J.'s manicured lawn. She decided her only chance was to reach the safety of the house and she ran even faster.

Hearing footsteps approaching behind her, she began screaming. She couldn't let the kidnappers take her again. She instinctively knew she wouldn't survive that ordeal twice.

The footsteps were gaining on her.

"Kaden!"

The door slammed open and he came running outside. He sprinted toward her as she ran toward him. She had unwittingly placed him in danger with her recklessness. Sawyer ran as the man chased her with a gun. Kaden was unarmed, but that didn't stop him from coming to her rescue. She picked up speed at the fear she had placed him in danger.

"Get to the house and lock the door," he yelled as he rushed past her.

She kept running, hearing the heavy thump of bodies colliding; however, Sawyer didn't stop until she had finally reached the door, slamming and locking it behind her. Running to the window, she saw Kaden and another man fighting. She looked around the room for a phone, not knowing what else to do to help Kaden.

When she couldn't find one, she turned back to the window, seeing Kaden slamming his fist into the man's face over and over. He tore the gun from the man's hand then brought it down on his skull until he lay still on the ground.

The security guard ran to Kaden, pulling him off the limp body before tossing the intruder onto his stomach and handcuffing his hands behind his back. Kaden then got to his feet. Sawyer saw him speaking with the security guard before he turned and headed back toward the house, his face a mask of fury. Sawyer stood by the window until the hard slam of his fist hit the doorframe.

She went to the door, her fingers fumbling with the lock until the door finally opened and Kaden brushed angrily by her.

"What the fuck were you doing out there?"

Shocked and still frightened by her narrow escape, she had trouble getting the words out. "I—I just wa—wanted t—to go f—for a walk." She was relieved when she finally managed to get the sentence out.

"You almost managed to get yourself kidnapped, Sawyer. Is that what you wanted?"

"N—n—no!"

"Why were you so close to the road?"

"I—I wanted t—to g—o—go for... a... walk." Sawyer took a deep breath, trying to get her stuttering back under control. It had been years since she had stuttered this badly. The years of speech therapy came back to her and she tried to gather her thoughts to gain control of her speech while Kaden stared at her as if she were crazy.

Sawyer belatedly realized it hadn't been a wise decision. She had almost got herself kidnapped, and both Kaden and the security guard hurt.

"Go to your room, Sawyer. I'll be up in a few minutes, but first I have to calm down. I told you not to leave the house, didn't I?" Kaden said harshly.

"Yes, but I was only going for a walk." She was proud of herself for not stuttering, but the way Kaden was gritting his teeth had her wishing she had remained silent.

"Go. Now. Before I paddle your ass here and now, without caring someone could walk in."

"You're not going to lay a hand on me." Fire blazed out of her eyes.

"Do you fucking realize that Mike was shot in his shoulder?"

"W—what... I—I didn't... know."

"Well, now you do. Not only that, but he could have been killed, so could you and I." By the time he referred to her, he was yelling.

Sawyer decided it was better to retreat to her room and give him a chance to calm down. She threw him a dirty look before she left though, which also wasn't the smartest move; he made a move toward her, but her fleeing footsteps managed to satisfy him temporarily.

Sawyer slammed the door to her room. Too wired to sit down, she walked back and forth across the carpet, talking to herself, calling Kaden various names as they came to her. It was only when she really became inventive that she realized how childish she was being. Her shoulders slumped as she began feeling terrible that the security guard had gotten hurt. Kaden also had a bruise on his cheekbone where he had been struck.

She had been warned twice not to be in front of the house and she had ignored it both times. Her defiance of Kaden's orders, when they had been made to protect her, caused a sick feeling in her stomach. He had been thrown into this situation because of her, and she had done nothing except give him trouble since the beginning.

Without his help, Sawyer knew her life would be one of hell, not living in luxury with a rock star trying to make her happy. He had tried to appease her about staying with the band and giving her a large sum of money, furnished her with expensive clothes, and even given her control of the kitchen, trying to relieve her boredom.

Sawyer's head swung toward the doorway when the door opened, and Kaden came in with a hard expression. Sawyer swallowed hard.

"Take your clothes off, Sawyer."

Sawyer started to refuse, but saw from his expression that he would take them off himself. She toed off her shoes then took off her jeans and t-shirt, standing before him in only her panties and bra.

"Everything."

Sawyer bit down on her trembling lip and reached back, unsnapping her bra and letting it fall to the building pile of clothing at her feet. She slid her panties down her hips, removing them also.

"Fold your clothes and place them on the chair."

Sawyer almost baulked at his commands, but bent over and picked up her clothes and shoes. Folding them, she placed them neatly on the chair before turning back to Kaden.

She forced herself to stand still as his eyes swept her body. His eyes narrowed on the nest of curls between her thighs. "Did you shower when you came upstairs?"

Sawyer had remembered what he had wanted her to do,

but she had ignored it when she showered. "Yes."

"So, if you had taken the time to spend doing what I wanted you to do, you wouldn't have been outside wandering around, almost getting kidnapped?"

"I didn't need to shave myself there because I'm not going to fuck you again," she explained.

"Yes, Sawyer, you are. You can bury your head in the sand and ignore what's going on here all you want. Tell yourself that each and every time I fuck you, Sawyer, if it makes you happy. But in the end, you'll still be fucked."

"I'll take your punishment this time because I deserve it, Kaden, but this," her hand went back and forth between them, "isn't going to happen again."

Kaden's eyes swept the room, landing on her dresser.

"Hand me your brush."

Sawyer tensed, knowing she had ignited his temper again, wishing she would learn to keep her big mouth closed. She was making a bad habit of challenging him when she was naked. Being stubborn wasn't going to win her any battles.

Defiantly going to the dresser, determined to see this through, she picked up the brush and handed it to him with sparks shooting from her eyes.

"Lean over the bed."

Sawyer began to regret her decision to give in gracefully; however, she obediently went to the side of the bed.

"Lean over. Place your hands one on top of the other."

Sawyer followed his instructions as heat began warming her pussy at being exposed to his gaze. Sawyer wanted to climb into the bed and cover herself, yet did as he asked.

"Spread your legs."

He was freaking turning her on, yet Sawyer became scared bone-deep in her body that she was enjoying this.

The first smack from the back of the brush against her ass had her tensing and standing straight up, disenchanting her about enjoying being punished.

"You just earned yourself two more for breaking position, Sawyer."

Sawyer resumed the position he required, cursing him mentally.

The second and third strokes of the brush had a heated warmth spreading across her butt. Four more strokes had tears welling in her eyes and her body clenching in need. Sawyer moved to adjust her position slightly.

"Stay still. I already can see you're wet, Sawyer. Don't think you can hide it from me."

Sawyer's legs went back to their original position, and she received two more strokes from the brush.

"What have you got to say to me, Sawyer?"

"I'm sorry," she mumbled.

"What did you say?" The brush landed against her ass harder than all the other times combined. It was then that she realized he had been taking it easy on her.

"I'm sorry." This time her voice was firmer and louder.

"Good girl."

Instead of the brush against her ass once more, she felt his finger part her pussy, sliding along her crease, stroking and spreading the wetness he found before his finger penetrated her opening and slid in deep.

The brush landed against her ass once again, jerking her backwards, driving his finger further inside her wet warmth. Sawyer wanted to scream; but instead, she maintained her position, afraid he would stop.

He gave her another finger as a reward and began pumping inside her harder as the brush lightly tapped her skin. Sawyer thought her knees would give out before she could come. She whimpered when Kaden removed his fingers; she needed him to finish what he had started.

"Do you want my dick, Sawyer?"

Sawyer felt herself on the precipice of wanting to tell him no; however, she said what her body was demanding.

"Yes," Sawyer admitted to herself and him.

"Then ask me nicely."

Sawyer knew what he wanted to hear. "Please, Kaden. I want your dick."

She heard the metallic noise of him unzipping his jeans then the slick feel of his cock as he placed it against her opening. He thrust hard into her, almost making her lose her balance, but she held still, letting him take her the way he demanded. His hand buried in her tumbled curls, bringing her head up as he leaned over her back.

"What am I doing, Sawyer?"

"You're fucking me," Sawyer gasped.

"That's right, and you're going to let me anytime I want, aren't you, Sawyer?"

"Yes." She barely managed to stifle her scream of pleasure as he thrust so high inside her that she was almost unable to cope with the pleasure taking over her body. She thrust back against him.

"Stand still. This time you're going to take what I give you."

He rose back up, grabbing her hips to steady her and then pounded inside of her. The sound filled the room as she took everything he gave her, wanting more.

A broken whimper passed her lips just before the brush landed with another smack against her ass. Pleasure exploded in her as Sawyer climaxed. Her clenching pussy tried to hold him within her as Kaden kept thrusting. She trembled under his controlling body. His hand slid from her hip to the front of her pussy where he found her clit, stroking her, drawing out the climax until she was shuddering uncontrollably.

"The next time I tell you to shave yourself, you'll fucking do it. Do you understand me?"

"Yes."

The brush landed against her harder and firmer.

"Yes, sir," Sawyer wailed.

"That's my girl."

Kaden brushed her clit again, and this time her hands and knees gave out and she landed on the bed as Kaden's cock jerked out his release deep within her.

He gently picked her up, lying her back down on the bed with her head on the pillow. He left her for a few minutes before returning. He spread her legs, cleaning her while he ignored her swatting hand.

"Stop it, Sawyer, or I'll get the brush and teach you the hard way to stay still."

Sawyer's hand immediately returned to her side. When he finished, he went back into the bathroom and Sawyer used the opportunity to cover herself with the sheet.

Kaden noticed when he returned to the room. He stood by the bed, removing his clothes and placing them on the chair beside hers, before sliding into the bed.

Sawyer started to say something then closed her mouth at his sharp look. Her ass was still burning and she wasn't anxious for another swat.

When he lay on his side, pulling her toward him, Sawyer tensed, not feeling comfortable close to his warmth. She preferred having her space, but she let him hold her, his arm wrapping around her waist with his hand on her breast.

"Go to sleep, Sawyer."

"Quit ordering me around," she snapped back sleepily.

His quiet laughter almost made her want to pick a fight, but she was too tired and too sore to face the consequences if she made him angry. She would teach the domineering bastard tomorrow that she wasn't going to become a pushover to his every demand.

Chapter Thirteen

Sawyer managed to sneak out of bed without waking Kaden. As she ran water in the oversized tub, she saw several bath bombs sitting on the shelf above the bath. Reaching up, she inquisitively sniffed a few before finding a faint vanilla scent she liked that wasn't overpowering.

She dropped the bath bomb into the tub, watching the bubbles and foam appear. She grinned as she enjoyed the treat. Vida and she stayed on a tight budget and wouldn't splurge on small extravagances.

Sinking into the warm water, she relished the warmth and the silky feel of the water against her skin. As she settled, she adjusted her butt so she wasn't putting weight on the sorest part of her bottom.

Taking the sponge, she appreciated being able to relax and take her time for the first moment in her life, to actually spoil herself. She shaved her legs and underarms. Glancing down, she couldn't bring herself to do as Kaden had suggested, so she laid the razor down, relaxing back against the side of the tub.

It wasn't long before the opening door had her head turning to see Kaden coming into the room.

"Get out," Sawyer said between gritted teeth.

Coming to a stop, Kaden asked, "Why?"

"Why?" Sawyer repeated his words. "I'm taking a bath."

"I can see that," he said with his eyes on her breasts.

"Get out." This time he gave her a full-fledged smile before going to the toilet and raising the lid before relieving himself. When he was done, he flushed and went to the sink to wash his hands.

Sawyer sat with her mouth open at the gall of the man to not wait until she was finished. When he turned back around, she couldn't hold back her response. "At least you raised the lid."

"I try to be a gentleman."

"A gentleman would be the last word I would use to describe you," she snapped.

"Really? I think I've been very gentle with you, Sawyer, despite your constantly defiant attitude toward me." Kaden sat down on the side of the tub, unconcerned with his nakedness.

Sawyer wanted to throw her bath sponge at him; but instead, she sat up in the tub, covering her breasts with the bright pink sponge.

His eyes fell to the razor lying on the side of the tub. "Tell me, Sawyer, if my hand was to dip into the water, would I find your pussy the way I have asked for it twice?"

Sawyer paled, lowering her lashes to cover her eyes. She wasn't frightened of Kaden, but neither was she anxious for her ass to be on the receiving end of another spanking so soon while it was still pink and sore.

Her silence showed her guilt.

Kaden stood up, looking down at her. "Since you couldn't follow my directions, I'm going to my room, instead of getting in the tub with you, which is what I wanted to do. I'll leave you to bathe alone." Sawyer saw the disappointment in his eyes and swallowed back the unnecessary remorse the bastard was trying to make her feel.

"If I knew your bottom wasn't still sore with being spanked for the first time, I would show you how ill advised you are for not listening to me, Sawyer. I expect you to take care of this act of defiance on your part immediately. Do you understand me?"

Sawyer nodded instead of cussing him out, which she thought was the wisest move on her part. Her nipples tightened, peeking out from behind the sponge. The freaking asshole could arouse her without laying a hand on her.

Kaden turned back before going out the doorway. "And, Sawyer, I expect you to find a way to make this up to me tonight."

She would make it up to him tonight all right; she would kill the freaking bastard before she ripped out his heart.

* * *

Jordan had managed to make breakfast for everyone. The eggs were still runny and the bacon burnt, but they were edible, so Sawyer managed to eat enough to stop her stomach from rumbling. She had just finished drinking the last of her coffee when Kaden came into the kitchen.

"Have you finished eating breakfast?"

"Yes."

"Good. Let's go then." He took her hand, ushering her out of the kitchen under Jordan's amused gaze.

"Where are we going?"

"I thought you'd like to get out of the house for a while and explore the town. I have items to pick up." Sawyer couldn't believe that she would willingly spend time with Kaden, but the idea of sitting around another day in R.J.'s house, bored to tears, stopped any protest she would have made.

Outside, instead of a car waiting, she saw a motorcycle parked in the driveway.

She was shocked when he led her to it and handed her

a helmet to put on.

She looked at it in bemusement. "I've never ridden on a motorcycle before," she said in awe.

"Scared?" he asked, climbing on to the huge machine.

"Hell no." Sawyer put on the helmet, grinning. She eagerly climbed on behind Kaden and wrapped her arms around him like she'd seen in the movies. He looked back, smiling at her enthusiasm.

He started the bike, yelling back. "Hang on." The bike roared down the driveway, and Kaden waved to the security guard on duty as they passed.

As they pulled out onto the street, Sawyer noticed a black explorer with Alec behind the wheel and several of his men inside. Alec followed behind as Kaden drove the bike expertly, keeping his speed down so that Alec could keep up.

When they reached town, Kaden pulled into the parking lot of a small shopping center. The store was tucked between a tattoo shop and a lingerie shop. Sawyer got off the bike as Kaden waited for her. Giving him a curious look, she wondered which shop he was going to. As they walked closer, she saw the one he was heading for was named Naughty Playground.

She was stumped until she drew closer to the sign on the door and saw that a whip outlined the letters on the sign.

"Hell no," Sawyer said, turning around. She saw Alec and his men waiting inside their vehicle, staring at them. So help her God, if any of them grinned at her, she would kill Kaden.

"Sawyer." Kaden drew her attention back to him. "You have ten minutes while I wait out here to go in and find what you want me to use when I punish you. I'm not fond of using a hair brush. If you don't find something appropriate in ten minutes, I'll come in and you won't be happy with my choice. Talk back to me and I'll go inside and make my choice and you'll really be unhappy." Kaden reached into his pocket and pulled out some cash, handing it to her. He then crossed his arms over his chest.

Sawyer hesitated.

"Tick Tock," Kaden said.

Sawyer opened the door, rushing inside the store where the startled female clerk jumped at her entrance. Sawyer's dazed eyes took in the store and knew she wouldn't find what she was looking for in time.

"A—ah, where are the umm... I... the—I guess they're called paddles?" Sawyer asked, confused on about what exactly what to ask for.

The woman came out from behind the counter. Seeing Kaden standing outside the doors, her lips firmed to hide her amusement. Sawyer appreciated the effort, but she was in a hurry.

"I'm kind of in a r—rush."

"They're over here."

Sawyer followed the clerk dressed in leather leggings and a shirt with no sleeves. The top dipped, showing her cleavage.

The woman stopped in front of a display, showing different paddles of different sizes and material. Some were rubber;, some were plastic and some were wood.

"I don't suppose you would happen to know which hurts the least, would you?"

The woman reached out, taking a black paddle that wasn't as thick or thin as the others. "This one isn't too bad," she said conspiratorially.

Sawyer reluctantly took it from her hand and then turned toward the cash register. A sudden thought had her turning back. She asked, "Is there something else besides paddles men use, which hurts even less than this?"

This time, the woman didn't try to hide her amusement. Walking to the next aisle over, she pulled down a box. Opening it, she showed Sawyer a small handle with several lashes. "It's a flogger, it looks scary, but it doesn't hurt at all compared to the paddle. It's made of deerskin. Women love this one because it makes the men feel all Dom while it arouses the women. Just don't forget to yell and scream. Got to make them think it actually hurts." She gave her a conspiring wink.

Sawyer grabbed it out of her hand, handing the paddle back to her. Going to the register, she paid for it with the cash Kaden had given her. She wasn't going to give him his change back, either. He deserved to lose it for embarrassing her.

She thanked the clerk and then went back out the door with two minutes to spare, proud of her accomplishment.

Kaden held his hand out for the bag, and Sawyer handed it to him. Deciding to take the clerk's advice to heart, she managed to fake a look of fear as he opened the bag. When he reached inside the bag to open the box, Sawyer still didn't worry until he looked back at her, closing the bag.

Handing it back to her, he said, "Wait here."

With that, he went inside the store. Sawyer watched through the glass door as he spoke to the clerk then saw her rushing down the first aisle, returning with the original paddle she had given her. Kaden shook his head no, saying something that had the woman dropping her eyes and rushing back down the aisle, quickly returning with a larger, red paddle. The rat bastard had known it was a fake prop and wasn't letting her get away with it. Sawyer watched as he went down another aisle, picking up several items, which she couldn't see, before paying the clerk. Her stomach clenched when the clerk gave her a look of sympathy as Kaden left the shop.

"Let's get some lunch," Kaden said, seeming in a much better mood.

Sawyer followed him back to the motorcycle, watching as he put his purchases into a saddlebag before placing hers in also. Getting on the bike, he turned the motor on as he waited for her to get on.

"Don't pout. I gave you fair warning, Sawyer. As soon

as you learn that I'm the one with the balls, you might actually have some fun."

"I doubt it," she said grumpily, putting on a helmet. This time, her arms circled him less enthusiastically.

Kaden pulled out of the parking lot, driving several blocks before he pulled over at another strip mall. This mall seemed more respectable, and she didn't hesitate to follow him inside the well known department store. She watched as he picked out several items, sometimes even asking her opinion. He chose commonsense items the guys were constantly fighting over on the bus, such as a new pair of shoes for Ax because he had forgotten his favorite pair in a hotel room. Several t-shirts for Sin since he ripped his off constantly when he was on stage. Then underwear for D-mon because Kaden said he was tired of seeing his junk on display.

"Maybe he just likes to show off."

Kaden laughed at her joke. "It's hard living on the road. If we don't replace the essentials, then they start stealing them off each other. If Ax swipes another pair of my socks, I'm going to hurt him."

He bought R.J.'s wife a set of cookware as a hostess gift. Obviously, he had noticed Jordan was systemically destroying their current set.

"Do you need anything?" he offered.

"Yes, Please." Sawyer went to the aisle she needed, picking up a package.

"I see my socks aren't the only ones that Ax has been pilfering," Kaden said when she laid the large pack of socks on the counter.

"Anything else?" He questioned.

She looked up at Kaden. "Thanks for getting me out of the house. I'm enjoying myself." Sawyer spoke the truth. She *was* enjoying herself, except for having to buy the paddle.

"You can give me a present tonight to reward me," Kaden's wicked voice whispered into her ear as he put his arm around her shoulder, pulling her to his side as they checked out.

Going outside, the sunny sky lifted her spirits even further. She began to feel like she was leading a normal life for the first time in months. Kaden took her hand, leading her to a restaurant at the end of the mall. The steakhouse was full, but they managed to find a seat without waiting.

The food was good. She finished all of it. Relaxing, Sawyer leaned back in her seat, drinking the last of her wine. She enjoyed spending time with Kaden when he was like this, engaging without being bossy. He had a quick sense of humor, but it could disappear in a second when something irritated him.

The booth next to them had two small children, and the mother was trying to unsuccessfully to soothe the infant. Kaden paid the bill, casting annoyed looks at the couple.

"Sorry," the mother said apologetically.

"There's no need to be sorry. No one can control a fussy baby. Try rubbing one of the ice cubes on her gums; she's the age they can become pretty fussy when they're teething."

The mother did as Sawyer had advised and the baby was soon playing with her rattle. As Kaden rose to leave, she thanked Sawyer. Sawyer smiled, following Kaden's fast stride.

"What's the hurry?" Sawyer asked once they were outside.

"I can't stand to be around babies," Kaden said, walking to his motorcycle.

"I figured that out myself when you said you had a vasectomy," Sawyer retorted, climbing onto the bike behind him. He didn't reply to her comment as he drove the bike out into traffic.

Their last stop was a liquor store, where Kaden bought several bottles of expensive wines. Alec came inside and carried them out to the vehicle he was driving.

Sawyer stood to the side while Kaden paid the bill, spotting a donation box for the needy. She counted out the money in her pocket that she had left from the money Kaden had given her earlier, slipping all of the money into the box. Turning away, she saw that Kaden had been watching her.

"Why did you give up your only cash?" Kaden asked.

"I wanted to," Sawyer said softly. Kaden's eyes searched hers before he pulled her close.

"Sometimes I can be a dick." She knew he was referring to his behavior at the restaurant.

"I know."

"Let's head back." He smiled ruefully at her acceptance of his flaw.

"Okay."

They rode back to R.J.'s home in silence. The roads on their return were busy. It was getting late in the day and workers were going home to their families. Sawyer's heart ached; she missed Vida so badly and hoped her friend was safe in King's care.

Chapter Fourteen

Sawyer went into the kitchen where she found Jordan completely overwhelmed. She felt guilty for leaving her when she knew R.J. had planned to have a dinner party.

"I'm sorry. I should have asked Kaden to bring me back sooner," she apologized.

"Don't you dare apologize. It's not your fault that I'm a terrible cook."

Sawyer looked around, seeing the haphazard way she was preparing the meal. Thankfully, she hadn't put the roast in yet.

"You can do the salad and get it ready, but go out and tell Kaden to serve everyone wine to keep them busy for twenty minutes."

"Me?" Jordan wasn't anxious to speak with Kaden.

"It's okay; he won't bite," Sawyer assured her, getting busy seasoning the roast and placing it in the oven. Hastily, she went to the refrigerator. Thankfully, she'd had the good sense to throw together a Brussels' sprouts gratin, and so she slid that in the oven also.

Jordan came back with a relieved smile and began cutting up the salad. Moving to the side, Sawyer made a quick dessert that wasn't fancy, but would taste good. She would wait until the roast was done before she placed it in the oven.

She helped Jordan plate the salads and told her how to plate the food. Seeing the young woman had regained control and that a young man had entered to serve the food, Sawyer went outside to take a seat at the table, which was perfect timing because everyone was just taking their seats as well.

Sawyer went to take an empty seat on the other side of Alana, who was sitting down next to Kaden. Her butt wasn't allowed to hit the chair, however, before Kaden's voice sounded over the conversations going on in the room.

"That's Sawyer's chair, Alana." The model thin women looked angry, but she didn't say anything as she moved to the chair Sawyer had been about to take. Sawyer controlled her embarrassed reaction at being made the center of attention, sliding into the chair Kaden was now holding out for her.

The waiter served the meal, and Sawyer was rewarded for her efforts when R.J. called Jordan out, complimenting her on the food. Sawyer winked at the young woman before she went back into the kitchen. Kaden raised a brow at her, yet he didn't comment.

After dinner, everyone went back into the living room, drinking the wine that Kaden had purchased.

Sawyer sat down on the sofa and Kaden sat down next to her. She was surprised he was making it obvious that they had become intimate, then realized when Sin pulled Megan down onto his lap, that none of the men took their relationships with the women in the room seriously. Even the woman who made no effort to hide she was in love with Ax was only considered a part time girlfriend. Ax had told her himself that he didn't want to be tied down and that Justine was just a good friend. Sawyer felt sorry for the woman, seeing from the look in her eyes that she didn't consider herself just friends with Ax.

Alana and Megan both concentrated their flirtations on Sin, who seemed to appreciate having two women vying for his attention. Kaden placed his hand on her thigh as he talked to Alec. Sawyer was listening to their conversation about the security needed for their next concert stop, but lifted her eyes when she felt a concentrated stare on her.

Briana was laughing at something her husband had said; however, her gaze was fixed on Kaden's hand on her thigh. Kaden drew her attention when he asked Alec if he had heard any further news about Vida.

"King placed her with his other women in his club. No one is going to get by his security." Sawyer worried about her friend staying in the strip club. She could tell from Alec's expression he was hiding something from her.

"A—are you sure she's okay?" Sawyer questioned him.

"I'm sure. There's not any trouble she can't handle." Alec stifled a smile when Kaden threw him a warning glance at his words. Not getting the unsaid joke and frustrated with the two men's attitude, she rose from the couch.

"I'm going to bed," she snapped. She maneuvered herself away from the couch they were sitting on. She was just a few feet away when she heard Kaden's voice.

"Don't forget my present, Sawyer." Sawyer kept walking, as if she hadn't heard the arrogant prick. Walking up the steps, she went into her bedroom and locked the door behind her.

"Payback is a bitch," she said sarcastically.

* * *

Sawyer woke up alone in her bed the next morning. While not exactly regretting her decision, she had woken with her body feeling needy. Sawyer didn't appreciate her body betraying her needs. While she had gone most of her life without a sexual partner, one night with Kaden and her body was giving her hell.

She would be better off with Vida, surrounded by

women, instead of a band full of men determined to show off their sexual prowess.

She took a shower before getting dressed in her only other pair of jeans, reminding herself that she needed to wash clothes today if they were leaving on the bus tomorrow.

Going downstairs, she walked into the kitchen where a strange woman was sitting at the table drinking a cup of coffee.

The woman rose from the table. "My name is Lucy. How may I help you?"

"Where's Jordan?"

"Ms. Jordan left; her trial period was over." Jordan had told her she would be leaving at the end of the week, but somehow she had thought she would be leaving early tomorrow morning when they left. She hadn't even said goodbye to her. Sawyer felt sad to have missed her; she had begun to consider her a friend.

"Oh. I'm sorry I missed her. I'll just pour myself a cup of coffee."

"Allow me." The woman efficiently poured her some coffee. "Would you like any breakfast?"

"I was just going to make myself a piece of toast." The woman moved around the kitchen and then a plate of toast with butter was handed to her.

"T—thank you." Feeling uncomfortable, she sensed this woman had no intention of getting friendly with one of R.J.'s guests. Not wanting to sit in the large dining room, she went outside to eat her toast by the pool.

It seemed like Kaden and Briana had the same idea; they were sitting at one of the tables. As she drew closer, she saw that Briana looked upset while Kaden's face was an expressionless mask behind his sunglasses.

She wanted to retreat when she saw them, but didn't want to appear intimidated. Instead, she sat down on one of the lounge chairs, setting her coffee on the small table next to it. She leaned back against the cushions as both of them continued quietly talking, ignoring her presence.

It wasn't long before Megan, Alana and Justine came outside wearing skimpy swimsuits. The women jumped into the water, screaming playfully, trying to draw attention to themselves. Alana and Megan actually removed their tops, throwing them to the side of the pool.

Disgusted, Sawyer was about to get up and go back inside the house when Alana got out of the water. Picking up a towel, she dried her body off before dropping the towel down on one of the empty lounge chairs. Going up behind Kaden, she placed her arms around his neck, and pressed her bare breasts against his back. One hand slid down his chest until her hand landed on his cock covered by his swimsuit briefs.

A knife stabbed in her heart as she watched Briana's chair screech back from the table, leaving Kaden sitting at the table with his cock in Alana's hand. Sawyer rose to her feet, determined to follow Briana's example.

"Sawyer, come here." Kaden's harsh voice had her freezing in place; her disbelieving gaze flew to his. "Come here, now."

Sawyer found her feet reluctantly carrying her toward Kaden. She couldn't seem to tear her gaze away from him as she stopped a few feet away, unable to force herself to go any closer.

"Did you deliberately lock your door against me last night?"

Sawyer licked her dry lips. "Y—Yes."

"I thought so. I wanted to give you the benefit of the doubt, but I can see you're determined to disobey me."

"Kaden, forget about her. Let's go to my room." Alana made no effort to lower her voice.

"Were you happy with your decision to lock me out?" His eyes dared her to lie.

"Nnn—no," Sawyer admitted honestly.

Kaden reached out, taking Alana's wrist in his hand and jerking her down in front of him. "Do not touch me again.

I do not fucking want your hand or your tits on me again."

"Okay, Kaden, I was just playing around." The woman took a step back when Kaden released her.

"You need to pack your bags and get the fuck out of here, Alana. I'm tired of dealing with you." The woman left, running toward the house without even bothering to cover herself.

"I don't play games, Sawyer. I outgrew those years ago. Do you want me in your bed or not? I'm done dealing with your on and off switch, and before you open your smart-ass mouth, you better think twice because, depending on your answer, you'll either be staying here with a number of security or leaving on the bus tomorrow with me sharing the bedroom with you."

Sawyer stood in shock at his ultimatum. She knew she would be safe here for the next couple of months, safe from Rick and her building desire for Kaden, yet…

"Well?" he snapped, the cold glare of his sunglasses making her answer harder. "Which one are you going to do?"

"Go on the bus." Sawyer lowered her gaze from his.

"You understand, Sawyer, just how our relationship is going to work? I expect you to obey me in the bedroom at all times, and when we're not, then you will continue to obey me in matters that I consider important."

"How will I know the difference?"

"You find out the difference when my paddle is on your ass," he said unrelentingly.

Sawyer almost changed her mind about leaving. The only reason she didn't was her body craved his. Surely this first rush of excitement would soon be over. She remembered her first and only sexual relationship, and how it had quickly ran out of steam.

Her relationship with Kaden should fizzle out about the same time as their deal expired. She could spend the next two months exploring the country and enjoy a kind of sexual relationship that she'd thought never to experience.

"Okay." Sawyer made her voice firm and controlled her speech until she didn't stutter her reply.

"Now, you can go upstairs. I'll send your lunch and dinner upstairs."

"But I thought we could go out again today before we're cooped up on the bus," Sawyer protested.

"Why should I spend my day pleasing you when you didn't spend the night pleasing me?"

The bastard kind of had a point.

"Have you finished your breakfast?"

"Yes."

"Then there's no need to stay any longer. You can return to your room. I'll see you tonight. Oh, and Sawyer, I haven't forgotten you disobeyed me about shaving yesterday."

Sawyer nodded before leaving.

Going back to her bedroom, she heard Alana yelling from the room down the hall and R.J.'s voice soothing her anger.

Sawyer threw herself down on the bed, landing on an object she hadn't seen. Pulling the box out from under her, she opened it to find a small reading device. She spent the next few hours downloading samples and books, enjoying her surprising present from Kaden.

She only took a break from reading when Lucy brought her lunch. She read while she ate and then dozed off with it still in her hand.

She woke just as it started to get dark. Jumping out of bed, she took a bath, using another of the bath bombs. If she didn't quit going through them so fast, she would have to sneak them out of the other bathrooms. When she finished, she rubbed the body lotion on her body.

Going into the bedroom, she was going to slip on one of her gowns when she stopped. Instinctively, she knew how Kaden wanted her when he opened the door.

* * *

Sawyer stood by the bottom of the bed and held her

breath as the door opened. His ruthless expression did not change when he saw that she was naked. The door closed with a snap behind him.

"I see you finally did as I requested."

Sawyer nodded her head, unsure that she would be able to control her stutter. She had never felt more nervous in her life; butterflies were having a field day in her stomach.

Kaden came to a stop in front of her. "This isn't going to stop me from punishing you for disobeying me twice."

"I—I know."

"Take off my clothes."

Sawyer took a step forward. She was about to reach out when she hesitated. "May I touch you?"

"Yes."

Sawyer could tell from his pleased expression that she had approached him correctly.

She reached out, unbuttoning the blue shirt that he had left un-tucked from his jeans. Meticulously pulling the shirt from his shoulders, she was about to let it drop to the floor; however, she caught herself, folding it and placing it on the chair next to the bed. She unsnapped his jeans after he voluntarily took off his expensive shoes. Kaden was such a contradiction, being a complete hard-ass rocker with the tattoos, while having expensive tastes in clothes.

Sawyer unsnapped his jeans, pulling them down his hips and off each leg. She again folded them, placing them on the chair next to his shirt. Sawyer went back to stand in front of him, waiting nervously for his next command.

"Where is the bag with your paddle?" Sawyer slowly went to the bedside table and opened the drawer, before removing the bag he had handed her after their day out together.

"Did you open the bag?"

"No." Sawyer had been too wary of its contents.

"Good." Kaden opened the bag, first pulling out the flogger she had purchased. He walked to the trashcan by the bed and tossed it in. Sawyer personally thought that was overkill. He could have at least kept it for when she was good.

Next, he pulled out a small tube of something and lay it on the nightstand, then a jar of lotion and two smaller objects that she had no idea what they were. They formed a line across the small table. Lastly, he pulled out the dreaded paddle.

"Why are you being punished, Sawyer?"

"Because twice you gave me the opportunity to—to—to shave, and I didn't."

"That has earned you five. What else?"

"I locked my bedroom door."

"That earned you an additional five. What else?"

Sawyer's mind went blank.

"I called you an asshole?"

Kaden's eyes narrowed on her.

"No, but you earned yourself another one."

Damn. She couldn't remember anything else, and she wasn't going to keep throwing misdeeds out, earning points.

"When you came out to the pool this morning, did you greet me?" Not giving her the opportunity to respond, he continued, "When Alana touched me, did you respond? No. As you are mine, I am yours, and no one touches what's mine. If another man had touched you the way Alana touched me, do you think I would have just stood there?"

"N—n—no." Sawyer could tell from the look on his face what he would have done. "I'm sorry."

"That earned you ten." Sawyer doubted she would be able to stand being paddled with so many strokes.

"Kaden."

"Take your position, Sawyer." His voice showed her no sympathy. "When I'm finished, I expect you to be properly apologetic."

"Yes, Kaden."

Sawyer moved to the side of the bed, bending over to

place her hands on top of the bed, one on top of the other. She widened her stance, which arched her butt, giving him the perfect target.

"You will count each stroke, Sawyer. How many will I be giving you?"

"Twenty-one."

The first stroke of the paddle almost had her breaking position. The hairbrush was smaller and couldn't hit as much flesh; the paddle was wider and longer, having no trouble covering a larger area. The sting wasn't bad, so Sawyer relaxed into the strokes, counting each one off.

Each stroke of the paddle had her becoming increasingly aroused. She couldn't understand this part of herself, only knowing that each additional stroke ratcheted her arousal up another notch until she was burning for a more intimate touch from him. The more he withheld himself, the more she wanted him. It had become a challenge to her to win his approval so that she could win his touch as her reward.

The last two strokes were the hardest. Her butt was now warmer than when they'd begun. After he finished the last stroke, his hand rubbed over the tender flesh with a soft lotion that soothed the heated warmth and aroused her into almost breaking her position.

"Stay still," Kaden ordered.

Sawyer heard him go into the bathroom and run water before he came back.

"Face me, Sawyer." Sawyer straightened from the bed, turning around. His gaze searched her clear eyes. "You took your punishment. Now I expect you to show me your gratitude."

"Thank you, Kaden," Sawyer spoke quietly.

"You're welcome." The bastard was enjoying himself while her body was demanding he relieve the fire he had risen with each stroke of his paddle.

He waited, expecting more. His dick was hard and pointed upwards. Kaden wasn't as unaffected as he pretended. Sawyer suddenly knew exactly what to do. She went meekly to her knees in front of him.

Her gaze went seductively upwards. "May I touch you?"

This time his voice was hoarse. "Yes."

Sawyer reached out, touching his cock with the gentlest of touches as she stroked and explored the most intimate part of his body.

"Harder, Sawyer." Her hand began stroking him with a firm grip as Kaden's jaw tightened. She edged closer to him, opening her mouth to take him as deep as she felt comfortable, while her hand stroked and explored his heavy balls, and her tongue investigated every inch of him. She used her hand on his cock to control exactly how much she would take.

His hand burrowed into her hair as he began thrusting into her mouth with his cock. He was gentle with her as she became used to his length. Once he saw that she was having no trouble, he increased his thrusts, sliding more of himself inside.

Kaden's hand left her hair and went to her breast, his hand finding her already beaded nipple. Pressing the tender nub between his fingers, the slight sting of pain had her hand leaving his cock to take his hand away from her breast. He didn't let her hand move his, but he did stop pinching her breast and his other hand went to her hair, holding her steady as he slid another inch into her mouth. Her hand automatically went to return to his cock, but the pressure on her nipple increased.

Sawyer finally understood his message. Her hand dropped to her lap, letting Kaden have total control over the depth that he drove his cock into her mouth. She had to trust him, although it was hard to do. He was slightly rough, demanding more of her than she thought she could give him; however, when she relaxed and let him have the control he demanded, he eased the depth of his strokes, alternating so that she had ample opportunity to breathe.

Sawyer felt his cock lengthen just before he came. He didn't slow, expecting her to take him. Her knees squeezed together as she sought to relieve the burning pressure between her own thighs.

When Kaden finished, he took a step back. "Thank you, Sawyer. I accept your apology."

Sawyer felt a rush of pride that she had succeeded in pleasing Kaden. It was silly that her body responded to the dominance he exuded, but it did.

"It's time to go to bed, Sawyer. Do you need to go to the bathroom?"

Sawyer nodded her head, disappointed that he wasn't going to relieve her own frustrated desire. She hurriedly used the restroom before returning to the bedroom where Kaden was already in bed. Sawyer turned the light out before climbing in beside him. Her eyes watered; she was so on edge from being denied her own organism. Payback was a bitch, she thought. This time without the sarcasm.

His final lesson of the night was one she'd never forget. She had denied him the previous night, and Kaden believed the punishment should suit the crime. She had locked him out of her bedroom the previous night, denying his body an orgasm. He returned the same to her by not letting her have her own orgasm tonight.

His arm circled her waist, pulling her back to him, her ass pressed against his cock, letting her feel what she had been denied. He then held her close throughout the night. She tried to shift her body away from his, and each time, he reached out, trapping her close. Even in sleep, Kaden tried to keep her under his control, gradually Sawyer was able to slip a few inches away, falling into a light doze just as   dawn   covered   the   morning   sky.

Chapter Fifteen

"We missed you for Thanksgiving, Kaden." His mother's voice held no recriminations for his failure to show.

"I missed you all, too, Mom. Tatiana's family wanted to meet me with us just becoming engaged," Kaden explained, sitting in the back of the limo with a pretty blonde by his side.

"I know, son. How's she doing?" Kaden lifted the woman's hand, placing it on his lap.

"She's good. She decided to stay for a couple of weeks with her parents until we meet up at the cabin I rented us for Christmas. You guys getting ready? Remind Grace to bring everything the kids need. We'll be miles away from the nearest store."

"I'll remind her. Kaden, there's something you need to know..." His mother's voice lowered. *"Grace is expecting again and..."*

"Jeez, Mom, hasn't she ever heard of birth control?" Kaden adjusted his hips as the woman he picked up from a popular nightclub, unbuttoned his jeans and pulled his dick out with nimble fingers.

"Mom, I have to go. I have Sin and D-mon waiting for me. The two men sitting across from him bit back their laughter.

"Wait, Kaden—"

He disconnected the call as the woman slid his cock deep into her

126

mouth. He sucked in a breath as her experienced tongue swirled against his cock.

"Anything important going on?" Sin questioned, his eyes not lifting from the woman's mouth greedily sucking on Kaden's cock.

"No, same old bullshit. My sister is pregnant again, and Mom is probably worried about her. Remind me to have R.J. send them some extra cash next month." Kaden leaned his head back against the expensive leather, groaning.

"Come on, Kaden, don't be so stingy." Sin reached forward, maneuvering the woman until she was on the floor between the seats. D-mon reached down, sliding the short skirt she was wearing until her ass was exposed.

"Help yourself; I don't mind sharing," Kaden groaned.

Kaden turned off the water before stepping out of the shower. Drying off, he slung the towel towards the laundry basket before returning to the bedroom.

Sawyer was sleeping deeply. She had since he had let her roll away from his body. He had held her most of the night, waiting for her to fall asleep. It was only when he had loosened his hold, that she had managed to attain it.

He had left her body unfulfilled last night. She had been so primed he could have slid his dick into her with no foreplay. Her mind was fighting their attraction, but her body was more than willing to concede to his demands.

Her beautiful face looked tranquil in sleep, disguising the usually cautious way she watched him. He watched as her arm fell to her side, exposing the tattoo she had on the back of her wrist.

Freedom.

Sawyer reminded him of a fragile bird who constantly struggled against a gilded cage. Kaden had never seen anyone—male or female—so unaffected by wealth. The clothes that R.J. had purchased from a local discount store were the ones she constantly wore, ignoring the expensive ones in her closet. Even the extra cash she had that he had wanted to make sure she kept on her, she had donated to the less fortunate. The woman had no self-preservation instinct. Sawyer hated to be waited on and cared for, preferring to do it herself. The only thing he could see she enjoyed was fucking bath bombs.

Kaden sat down on the mattress beside her hip. He couldn't tie her to him emotionally; she was too guarded for that. He wondered, not for the first time, if it was something from her past or her kidnapping by Redman that was responsible for her behavior. Sexually, he could reach her, but if he attempted to draw her emotionally closer, she shut him out. Sadly for her, he had no compunction using his more experienced skills against her. He wanted her that badly.

He lowered the sheet, exposing her body before sliding between her thighs. He eased his cock into her tight pussy as her thighs rose, clamping against his hips as he thrust in and out of her.

"Fuck me," he whispered into her ear.

Her hips began thrusting back against him, giving them both what they needed. When her eyes sleepily opened, the clear, golden depths stared up at him, making no effort to hide her arousal.

His hand reached down between her thighs, finding her clit before rubbing the delicate bud until he had her arching and thrusting up harder against him. "This is my cunt."

Pounding inside her, his hand left her clit to raise both of her thighs higher, spreading her wider. He leaned to his side and then reached for the tiny rings on the nightstand he had placed there last night. He laid one on her nipple, tightening it until she gasped before doing the same to her other breast.

"These are my tits." He leaned down, licking the nubs being pinched by the nipple rings. "Next month, we're passing through a town where I know someone who pierces. You're going to let him pierce them for me."

Sawyer groaned at the way he was talking to her.

Her hands came to his side, grasping him as her legs slid up even higher with his hands pushing them up. Kaden rose above her as his cock moved in and out, with a driving need to climax. Kaden gritted his teeth, not wanting to come yet. He wanted to prolong the pleasure of taking her.

His mouth returned to her nipple, biting down, smiling when her scream filled the air. His mouth then went to her other nipple, and she was so primed that she screamed at the first brush of his lips against the red bud. No sooner had the scream ended than he rose up, pulling his cock from her pussy. Her whimpers of need almost had him giving in and returning to the silky depths.

"No, Kaden, don't stop." Sawyer reached out to him, but he forestalled her by flipping her onto her belly and sliding back between her thighs. He used his knees to separate her thighs wider before he raised her to her knees.

He reached for the last item on the nightstand. He opened the tube, smearing a generous amount on his cock before placing it back on the nightstand. He placed his cock against the tiny rosette peeking between the globes of her ass as his hand rubbed the still faintly pink globes.

"This is my ass."

Sawyer jumped, but he held her steady as he began to fuck her.

"Kaden!" Sawyer's voice sounded loud in the quiet room.

"Hush, Sawyer. You can take me." Kaden saw her hands grip the sheets beneath him as she struggled to do just that. Using steady pressure, he managed to slide his cock inside her.

"That's it; fuck back against me, Sawyer," Kaden coached her.

The timid movements of her hips spoke to her newness of the experience. Reaching around her, his fingers found her clit again, stroking her until she began to move back against him more forcefully.

"There is no part of your body that isn't mine to take anytime I want." Sawyer's only answer was to groan as he thrust his remaining length deep inside her ass.

Kaden reached over to the nightstand, knowing what she needed to bring her over the edge she was clinging to. The paddle came down on one pinked cheek, letting it linger before raising the paddle and coming down again even harder as he watched her ass clench on his cock. Her screams filled the room.

Kaden dropped the paddle to the floor, his hands going to her breasts to remove the nipple rings, tossing them to the nightstand before his hand returned to her breasts, rubbing them. He enjoyed her screams of pleasure as he drew out her climax to a torturous level. When she would have dropped to the mattress in exhaustion, he held her still.

"Only one of us is done, Sawyer." His hands tugged her backward onto him, using her tender breasts. When she was finally able to crawl out of this bed, there would be no doubt in her mind and body who she belonged to.

Kaden finally allowed his restraint to loosen, thrusting against her as he enjoyed the pleasure of having her beneath his body. Leaning backwards onto his calves, he pulled her back until she was against his chest.

His mouth to her ear, he said, "You are mine."

His fingers gently twisted her nipples until she gasped and repeated, "I'm yours."

"I'm yours," Kaden stated firmly.

"You are mine," she repeated, this time without his encouragement.

At her words, Kaden finally allowed himself to climax deep within her. When he finished, he reluctantly pulled out of her before helping her to lie down on the bed. He went to the bathroom and ran the bathtub full of hot water, throwing one of her bath bombs in before he returned to the bedroom and gently picked her up, carrying her to the tub. Carefully, he stepped in, holding her as he sat down and placed her between his thighs. She leaned back against him, groaning.

Kaden laughed, his hand skimming through the thick foam, massaging it into her skin.

"Kaden?"

He leaned back against the side of the tub, enjoying the peacefulness of the moment with her. "Hmm?" he said, stroking her back.

"I'm going to kill you."

Chapter Sixteen

I am on the edge of death, and death is taking over me.
Resuscitate me, I wanna breathe you in.
Resuscitate me, I wanna live again.

I am filled with a darkness. My veins now run black,
And only you can change that.
Resuscitate me, I wanna breathe you in.
Resuscitate me, I wanna live again.

Let your light take hold of me.
Get rid of this misery.

Time's running out. Give me one last shot.
Resuscitate me, I gotta breathe you in.
Resuscitate me, I gotta live again.

Sawyer stood behind the curtain as she listened to the song, grinning as Kaden turned to flash her a smile. The weeks on the road had been tiring, but she also had to admit that they had been the happiest of her life.

The only part that had kept her worried was Vida.

Kaden hadn't heard anything about her friend, but had confided that the FBI had warned Alec to add additional security measures. Alec had, and he had also remained by her side until she entered her bedroom on the bus.

The song ended, and another one started with Alyce walking seductively onto the stage. Her loose t-shirt hung low, exposing her black bra along with the areolas of her nipples. Her skintight booty shorts and thigh-high boots made Sawyer regret her decision yet again to remain in her own jeans and shirt. Each night she saw them together, she swore she wouldn't put herself through it again.

Tonight, they were in Michigan, and the band had been eyeing each other warily. When she had asked Kaden if anything was wrong, he had denied the way everyone was acting.

The performance finally over, Kaden and the band exited the stage. They had planned on spending the night in a hotel, but Kaden had insisted they push through to the next concert.

The VIP room was packed to capacity with several of the local contest winners still there. Sawyer leaned back against the wall, watching Kaden take several pictures with the local personalities when R.J. interrupted him, pulling him to the side.

She could tell he was becoming angry by the harsh look on his face. So, when he nodded and R.J. left the room, Sawyer wondered what was going on to make Kaden so angry. D-mon and Sin walked over to him. She could tell they were questioning him and whatever Kaden answered had them happy.

Noticing that Sawyer was watching, Kaden excused himself and came to her side. "R.J. just told me there's trouble with the bus. Apparently, it can't be fixed until tomorrow and we're going to have to stay the night at the hotel."

"That's fine. It'll be nice to get off the bus for a while." She knew Kaden preferred to stay on the bus because it was safer for her. However, it was making the band crazy. Both D-mon and Sin were scoping out the women in the room to share the night with; even Ax—the more conservative of the group—was looking over the available women.

"We'll leave in twenty. Alec is getting us some cars."

"Okay."

Kaden left her, returning to the press who were covering the concert. It was closer to thirty minutes later before they all slid into the limo. D-mon and Sin sat across from Kaden and her. Ax and R.J. rode in the other car with the women they had selected to spend the night with them. Sawyer had learned early on that R.J. would separate the band from the women to get the women to sign a privacy agreement. If they refused to sign, they didn't make it out of the limo and into the hotel room.

"Brings back memories, doesn't it, Kaden?" Sin asked while staring at her.

"There are some memories not worth repeating."

"You sure?" Sin asked.

Sawyer wondered what he was questioning.

"I'm sure." His arm slid over her shoulders, pulling her closer to his side.

"Shame. I was looking forward to it," Sin remarked, his eyes going down her body.

Sawyer stiffened against Kaden's side. Even she understood that look.

"Knock it off, Sin."

Sin grinned, shrugging his shoulders.

It didn't take long for them to reach the hotel where the limo pulled around back and they stayed seated until Alec opened the door.

Kaden stepped out, taking her hand as they followed the security detail to the back elevator. R.J. had rented them two connecting suites, calling ahead to have food waiting on them.

Feeling slightly nauseous from snacking on the finger

foods at the arena, Sawyer opened one of the trays, finding a succulent chicken breast with a mushroom gravy and fingerling potatoes. She had quickly figured out the one who grabbed the trays first got the best choice. After she had become stuck with burgers and fries several times, she had learned to become more assertive.

She had sat down at the table when Kaden came back from taking a shower, his hair still wet. Sawyer smiled up at him as he leaned down, placing a brief kiss on her lips.

"That looks good. Anymore left?"

"Nope. You shower, you lose," she joked. "Ax took three."

"He's a bottomless pit." He searched through the remaining trays, ending up with a chicken Alfredo pizza. "It could be worse."

"Yes, it could," she said, remembering getting stuck with oysters on the half shell.

They ate as the others finished eating. Sin and D-mon were pumped up with energy from the concert. Even Ax had brought a woman back for the night.

"Has the band played here often?"

"It's where our band formed," Kaden answered her question with a closed look on his face.

"Do you have family here in Michigan?" Sawyer asked, surprised none of them had made arraignments to see their families while in town.

"Not anymore. Ax, D-mon and Sin's families all moved to warmer climates." Kaden got up, taking their empty trays to the trolley. Sawyer didn't ask any more questions, sensing it was closed for discussion by Kaden's closed expression.

A knock sounded on the suite door, and Kaden went to answer it. Sawyer saw his back stiffen as he stepped aside, letting a woman enter the suite. Sawyer glanced around the room, seeing the same startled reaction from all the band members. Ax looked toward her before coming to stand next to her.

Sawyer recognized the exotic woman. Her and Vida might not have had the money for CDs, but magazines were cheap. You also didn't need to buy magazines to be able to recognize Tatiana Shepas; her famous face and body were on billboards and televisions everywhere.

She had dated two extremely popular actors. She had even become engaged a few years ago to a well-known rock star who had been famous almost from birth. She looked at Kaden, gripping the back of the chair so she didn't fall down. When he'd said he had walked away from the music industry for a few years, he hadn't been lying. It was five years to be exact.

She had always assumed he had been a part of Mouth2Mouth; it had never occurred to her that they hadn't gone by his band's original name. Cross was the lead singer of CrossWinds. They had dismantled and gone their separate ways when Cross's entire family had been killed in an airplane crash.

He had finished his concert tour then walked away. Tatiana had been interviewed constantly about his entering rehab. No one knew if it was drugs or sex addiction, which had put him there. Tatiana had remained silent through the entire ordeal.

She reached up, brushing her lips against Kaden's. He didn't step away when she hugged him, either. Her liquid brown eyes that she had become famous for showed she was still in love with him.

"Aren't you going to say hello, Kaden?" Her sultry voice carried in the suddenly quiet room.

"Tatiana," Kaden said, closing the door.

"Are you surprised? R.J. said he would help me surprise you."

R.J. stepped forward. "Hello, Tatiana. It's good to see you again."

"R.J." Tatiana brushed her cheek against his.

"I take it the bus is fine?" Kaden made the statement, looking toward R.J.

"We thought it might be better if she surprised you. It's downstairs," R.J. answered, revealing his deception.

Kaden remained quiet.

"Kaden, please don't be angry at R.J. I jumped at the chance to see you again. I wish you had called."

"R.J. called you?" Kaden asked sharply.

"Of course. I quit trying after the first two years, but I never forgot about you, Kaden. How could I?"

Sawyer was sickened by the woman's expression because it was the same one on her own face when she was around Kaden.

"Please, Kaden, can we talk in private?" Tatiana's pleading voice had Kaden's attention. Sawyer began to feel like a fifth wheel.

"You can use the other room." R.J. went to the connecting door, unlocking it. "It will give you both some privacy."

Tatiana walked through the doorway, casting Kaden another pleading glance.

"Give me a few minutes?" Kaden turned to Sawyer, who stared back at him numbly. She nodded her head, needing a few minutes to gather herself.

Kaden went into the other room and closed the door behind him at the same time that the room he had just vacated became silent; the other women were giving her sympathetic looks. Sawyer didn't need to be told what they thought. There was no comparison between herself and Tatiana.

"Well, that was a downer. Good job, R.J.," Ax said angrily.

"If they can resolve their issues, maybe he will come back full-time instead of walking away again when the tour ends. Isn't that what you want, Ax? You're never going to have the success with Jesse that you had with Kaden."

"Tatiana wasn't the reason he left and she won't be the reason he comes back," Sin said, standing up. "It's bullshit you pulled this stunt, R.J. You're never going to learn your lesson, are you?"

R.J. paled at Sin's words.

"I need to get my things out of the bus," Sawyer broke into the brewing fight. "Could you call Alec and ask him to send someone to escort me?"

"I'll take you," R.J. volunteered. "I need to grab my own clothes."

Ax touched her wrist as she passed him. "You all right?"

"I'm fine." It hurt that Kaden had left to talk to a woman he used to be engaged to, but she had done a good job so far not letting jealousy rule her and she wasn't going to start now.

Sawyer followed R.J. out the door. They waited in silence for the elevator, entering it when the door slid open.

"I didn't mean to cause problems between you and Kaden." He broke into the uncomfortable silence between them.

"Yes, you did." She had noticed that he had been constantly throwing women Kaden's way. Whenever R.J. picked women, he made sure to include a couple of extras; some she had even begun to notice resembled her.

R.J. didn't say anything else after Sawyer's comeback. They exited the elevator in strained silence where the bus was parked several feet from the back door.

"Maybe we should call Alec? Where are they anyway?" Sawyer said nervously.

"They're in their rooms. They've had even less space in their vehicles than we do on the bus. I was trying to give them a break, but if you prefer, I can call," he said, taking out his phone.

"N—no. That's o—okay. Alec usually leaves someone watching the door and bus, but I don't see anyone." Her eyes searched the darkened parking lot.

R.J. shrugged as he opened the door, holding it impatiently for her. Sawyer went out, feeling suddenly nervous; however, her eyes kept surveying the parking lot, seeing nothing out of the ordinary.

R.J. unlocked the bus and then waited for Sawyer to enter it first. She was up the first step when she knew she had made a terrible mistake leaving the hotel room. The light came on when R.J. flicked a switch.

Sawyer turned to escape, expecting R.J. to do the same. Instead, he blocked her, forcing her up the remaining two steps.

"Hello, Sawyer."

Chapter Seventeen

Rick was sitting in the leather chair by the window with two other men she recognized from when she had been kidnapped. The two security guards were lying on the floor, unconscious with their hands and feet tied.

Rick got to his feet, his fake charm apparent in his sleazy smile. How she had missed it when he had asked her out, she didn't understand.

He stepped in front of her, sliding his thumb down her cheek.

"You've led me a merry chase, Sawyer, but playtime is over. Morgan, bring the car around. We don't want Kaden showing up accidently." The man to Rick's left brushed by her as he went out the door.

Rick pulled out an envelope, tossing it to R.J. as headlights shown from outside, glaring into the bus.

"Let's move." Rick took her by the arm and she tried to jerk away.

Rick shook her until her teeth almost rattled. "Do not fuck with me, Sawyer. You have been a pain in my ass for months. If your boyfriend barges in this time, I'll kill him. Is that what you want?"

"N—n—n—no."

"Then move your ass." He threw her down the steps where Morgan caught her before she could fall. He held her tightly until Briggs slid into the backseat, pushing her in after him then sliding in himself, slamming the door closed.

Rick opened the driver's door, getting in behind the steering wheel. "See, Sawyer, how well things work out when you do as you're told? It's a lesson you need to remember."

Sawyer didn't look out the window as the bus and R.J. disappeared from view.

R.J. was a snake that had betrayed not only her, but also his friends who'd trusted him. Sawyer wasn't surprised by his duplicity; however, she feared that as long as R.J. stayed with the band, none of them were going to be safe.

* * *

"I think we've said all we need to say, Tatiana."

"I've missed you, Kaden," Tatiana's soft voice whispered between them. "Are you sure we can't start over? I've never stopped loving you."

"Tatiana, I'm with someone else now." Kaden's voice didn't soften

"When has that ever stopped you?" Kaden heard the bitterness in her voice.

"I need to get back to Sawyer. It was good to see you again. I should have called you and cleared the air a long time ago." Regret glimmered momentarily in his eyes before they hardened once again.

Kaden went to the door, opening it. He left her no choice other than to follow him, immediately going for the other door to show her out of the suite.

"Goodbye, Kaden." Tatiana paused in the doorway.

"Goodbye, Tatiana," he said, closing the door behind her. Ax, Sin and D-mon all stared at him, waiting for his reaction.

"Where's Sawyer?" he asked, searching the room for

her.

"She went to the bus twenty minutes ago to get her clothes. R.J. took her," Ax answered as he poured himself a glass of whiskey.

"Why not Alec?"

"We just assumed he had men outside; he always does," D-mon answered.

"She should have been back by now," Kaden said, becoming impatient.

"She's probably taking a few minutes to herself. She seemed pretty upset," Ax said, downing the whiskey in one swallow.

Reaching into his pocket, Kaden pulled out his cell phone. It began ringing before he could key in a number. He listened as R.J. yelled into the phone that Rick had been on the bus and taken Sawyer.

"Where's Alec?" Kaden tried to remain calm.

"In his room." He disconnected from R.J. quickly as he ran out the door, Sin, D-mon and Ax running out behind him.

"What's going on?" Sin asked.

"Rick has Sawyer." The elevator opened, and the men quickly filed in. Impatiently, Kaden pressed the ground floor.

"How the hell did he get her?" Ax asked.

"I don't know, but I'm going to find out." Kaden felt his heart in his throat. He hadn't felt this way since he had heard about the airplane crash. He had to find Sawyer; anything else was not an option.

* * *

It was two hours later before Alec came back onto the bus with information. The band was sitting around the room tensely waiting. The two security guards had been taken to the hospital and treated for concussions.

Alec stood at the front of the bus. "Rick has her. We're searching for her, but there isn't a trace of her yet. I notified the FBI and they are doing what they can. It

142

doesn't look good, Kaden. Whoever Rick works for, they are experienced at making women disappear."

"What if we offer him more money?" Kaden's voice was hoarse.

"I don't think it's a matter of money. From what I understand, he wants both Sawyer and her friend as leverage against his competition, but I'll make the call. How much do you want me to offer?"

"Whatever it takes."

Alec nodded, turning to R.J. "Do you want to make the call or should I?"

"What's that mean? Why would I want to contact him? He's not exactly answering my calls since this whole mess started," R.J.'s sarcastic voice held a tinge of fear.

"Don't lie, R.J." Alec pulled out his phone, tossing it to Kaden.

He caught it in his hand, seeing a video that had been recorded. Pressing play, Kaden watched as the two guards were led up the stairs with a gun on them. Rick's men efficiently knocking them out while he sat and watched. Kaden's hand tightened on the phone as he watched Sawyer and R.J. enter the bus then him block her escape. When he saw Rick toss the envelope, it was everything he could do to stand and watch the rest of the tape. R.J. watching as Rick shook Sawyer was the final straw; he lost what little reason he had left to remain in control. Lunging for R.J., he struck him with his fist, knocking him to the floor. Not stopping, Kaden kept hitting him until Ax and Sin managed to get him off their tour manager.

"I am going to kill you, R.J.," Kaden threatened.

Alec helped R.J. to his feet before disgustedly releasing him.

"I had to; Rick was threatening to tell Briana how much debt we were in. Do you know how much money we've lost since you left? Do you even care?" R.J. yelled.

"No, I don't. If Mouth2Mouth couldn't pay your bills, then you should have moved on to another band, but you couldn't, could you, R.J.? Everyone in the industry knows you can't keep from interfering in their lives. The only reason we've let it go was because we felt we owed you. After the stunt with the women at the start of the tour, you knew this was your final tour with us. Sin already told you last week. You greedy bastard. You sold Sawyer out. What kind of bastard does that?" D-mon grabbed R.J.'s shirt.

Ax pressed his hand on D-mon's chest, holding him back from hitting R.J.

"Stop it; this isn't helping to get Sawyer back." Kaden wrapped his hand around R.J.'s throat. "You better pray we get her back, because right now, I'm about to kill you. Alec, call Rick and try to negotiate a new deal. If he doesn't take it, try something else. I don't give a fuck what you have to say; get her back."

Kaden loosened his hold enough for R.J. to breathe and then turned to the only person he felt stood a chance of finding Sawyer with his connections. "I want this sack of shit off this bus and out of our lives, but first, I want the tapes he's held over my head for five years. Can you do that?"

"Yes, Kaden." Alec motioned two of his men who were waiting by the bus door to take R.J. away. "That I can do."

* * *

Sawyer saw the familiar scenery passing by, and her heart leapt for a second in joy until she realized there would be no happy reunion between her and Vida. She hadn't expected them to bring her back to Queen City. Somehow, she had thought that they would have killed her off or passed her along to another client by now.

Driving through town brought tears to her eyes. She would never have believed it possible, but she had been homesick for this city that she had tried for years to escape.

The car pulled into a garage that she was familiar with,

yet had never been inside. It was a local recording studio.
The car stopped and Morgan got out taking her arm. No
one was around as Briggs came to her other side and then
both men ushered her inside to an elevator.

As they waited for the elevator, Sawyer looked outside
the windows.

"It won't do you any good. They're bullet proof and
the door is controlled by security. No one gets in or out
without being buzzed in." They had their illegal system
down so there wasn't a chance of escape.

Sawyer stepped into the elevator when it opened, both
men by her side. Briggs pushed the button and the elevator
moved upwards. When they reached the top floor, they
guided her to a private office where Briggs rapped on the
door before opening it.

She recognized the man looking out the window as he
turned toward the door when it opened. He had become
known throughout her neighborhood and the seedier side
of Queen City. His name was Digger, and most people in
Queen City were afraid of him. The only one in town who
had been able to keep Digger under some control was
King, although he had been trying to steal King's power
the last couple of years.

"I see that you finally were able to accomplish what
you set out to do." His face was unexpectedly handsome,
but there was a cruel twist to his mouth. Sawyer shivered
when he looked her over as if she was less than human to
him.

"Sawyer, have a seat." Briggs pushed her toward the
chair in front of Digger's desk. Shakily, she took a seat.

"Now, you're going to be a smart woman and listen to
me before you open your mouth. You have some
information I want. You can tell me what I need to know
and I'll see to it that you can walk out that front door.
Don't tell me what I want to know and they'll carry you
out the back."

Sawyer twisted her hands together in her lap.

"Do you understand what I'm telling you?"

Sawyer knew she couldn't answer him without stuttering so she nodded her head.

"Good." Digger took a seat behind the large desk. "How well do you know King?"

"I—I don't," Sawyer spoke truthfully. She could tell by the look on his face he didn't believe her. "I s—s—s—saw him when I w—w—was a kid at my apartment building." Sawyer sucked in deep breaths, determined to get herself back under control. Relaxing her shoulders, she waited for his next question.

"Then why, when you were kids, did he extend his protection to cover you and Vida?"

"He extended it to Callie, Vida and me." Sawyer was proud of herself for managing to get out a sentence without stammering.

"Callie?"

"She was another girl from our complex." Sawyer saw no reason not to tell him. Callie was the only one beyond his reach.

"Why am I just now hearing about her?"

"Probably because she's dead," Sawyer said sarcastically. "She died when she was eight."

"Her mother and father?"

"Her mother died the same day and no one knew who her father was."

"Could it have been King?"

Sawyer could see that he thought he was getting somewhere. She took perverse pleasure in bursting his bubble. "No."

"How can you be so sure?"

"Brenda was not only a whore, but a slut. You know King; what do you think?"

Everyone in town knew that King didn't touch whores. He liked to sell their services, but he kept his pleasure away from business. When King played, he liked to pick women who were from upper society that felt they were getting a thrill by fucking someone of King's caliber. He got exhilarated by dragging them down to his level.

"Why did King extend his protection to you and your friends then?" Digger asked, leaning back in his expensive chair.

"I honestly don't know. I've thought about if off and on for years and couldn't figure it out." The ring of truth and confusion sounded in her voice.

"I see." Digger motioned to Briggs who was standing behind her. His hands circled her throat, squeezing tightly. Her hands went to his, trying to break his hold as she fought, trying to get away.

When she thought she was going to pass out, she heard Digger's voice through the buzzing in her ears. "That's enough."

Sawyer gasped for breath when Briggs released her, and Digger waited until she quit before he began questioning her again. "I suggest you think harder."

"Once, several boys ganged up on us, causing Callie and Vida to almost be hit by a car. I pulled them away from the road before they were hurt. That was the only contact we had with King."

Her hand went to her sore throat. "H—he wasn't my f—father, and he wasn't Vida's, s—so maybe he was protecting the driver of the vehicle? I—I don't know."

"How do you know he wasn't Vida's father?"

"B—because Goldie kept a picture of Vida's father on a s—shelf in her apartment. Vida showed it to me one time. He wasn't my father because my mother didn't even know King until I was two-years-old."

"That's all you know?"

"Yes."

"It's useless information."

"I don't know what else I can tell you. There isn't a connection between King and us."

"I am beginning to see that the problem for you is that the only reason you were useful to me was for information. Since you're useless, I have no further benefit by keeping you.

"Take her to the basement."

Chapter Eighteen

Sawyer lay on the bed, listening to the soft cries from the other rooms. She had lost track of the number of days she had been held in the tiny room. She was beginning to lose touch with reality. The only contact she had with the other women was being forced to listen to their misery.

So far they hadn't drugged her; that would defeat their purpose. Digger still believed that she knew something.

She was hungry. *I will never complain about eating at another buffet*, she thought wryly. She wiped a tear away. At least Vida was safe for now. Whoever was protecting her, frightened Digger. She had seen the wariness in his eyes when she'd heard him telling his men to back off when they grew tired of her lack of information and wanted to go after Vida.

A loud explosion had her sitting up on her cot, with terror swamping her. Running to the door, she put her ear to it, listening to every sound she could hear. She stepped away when she heard the sound of gunfire. She instinctively hid in the darkest corner of her room, crouched down and hiding in case any of Digger's men came for her.

She wanted to scream along with the other women, though she managed somehow to control herself, wanting more to be able to listen to what was happening in the building.

Another smaller explosion sounded closer.

Relief flooded her when she heard the FBI yell out. She started crying in relief at the sound of doors opening and women being set free. It had her running to the door, banging on it, afraid they would miss her. The sound of a key in the lock had her stepping back.

She started crying harder as the door swung open and an officer stood there with an FBI vest, who quickly ushered her up the steps with the other women. They kept reassuring them they were safe and free. As Sawyer brought up the rear with one of the officers behind her, she felt him lurch forward, causing her to fall to the ground as he landed heavily on her. She knew he had been shot when she felt his dead weight.

His body was thrown off her and she was jerked to her feet.

Digger's man, Morgan, had her by her arm, dragging her back the way she had just ran from. Smoke filled the air as she started screaming for help.

"Make another noise, and I'll kill you," Morgan grunted as he ran down a hallway, dragging her with him. He went around the corner, coming to a stop at the large man blocking their path with a gun in his hand. The man didn't hesitate. Before Morgan could even point his gun, he shot him. Morgan's hand fell away from her as he dropped to the ground where Sawyer looked down at him. A bullet hole was right between his eyes.

"Let's go, Sawyer." King held his hand out to her, his eyes unremorseful.

Sawyer gave him her hand, running with him toward another doorway. He paused before the door, and then pushed it open, keeping to the side of the building.

She glanced across the few feet where the whole

parking lot was filled with police and fire trucks as a car pulled up in front of them with its lights off. King opened the backdoor and pushed her in before getting in himself. The car pulled slowly out of the lot, heading away from the burning building and police.

"That's the most excitement I've had in a while." King's merciless appearance had not changed over the years. His large body with dark hair and eyes would make anyone hesitate to approach him. The cold-blooded way he handled his enemies sent them running. He was wearing dark jeans and a jacket, which was the most casual she had ever seen him; usually, he was wearing expensive suits.

His head turned toward her, studying her. "You've looked better, Sawyer."

Sawyer gave a wry laugh. "I've felt better. What's going on, King?"

"Digger was under the misguided impression that you have information about me that no one else knows." Sawyer broke eye contact with him, going to the extremely broad shoulders of the man driving the car.

"Is Vida okay?"

"Vida is doing extremely well. Your little friend is being watched by an acquaintance of mine."

Sawyer couldn't decide if that was good news or bad news, considering the caliber of friends King had.

As if reading her mind, King set her mind at rest. "Colton is a good guy. He'll take excellent care of her." He lifted her hand, turning it until her tattoo showed in the faint light. "I believe he was the one who gave you this tat." Sawyer remembered the man who had given her the tattoo years before. He wasn't someone that you forgot.

The car took a turn and Sawyer realized where they were going. "Why are we going to the airport?" Sawyer questioned.

"Because you need to stay out of town a little longer. The FBI managed to let Digger and Briggs slip from their grasp, and you're not safe in town until he's caught."

"But I want to see Vida!" Sawyer protested.

"Bad enough to get her killed?" He callously disregarded her protests. "Digger's operation might be hurt, but he's a long way from being out of business. Colton is more than capable of seeing to it that Vida is taken care of; however, Digger won't use his full strength against her unless he has to. You go running to her and you'll give him that reason. I can't just kill the bastard the way I want to. Because he's such a fuck up, the FBI are watching both of us."

The car passed through a private gate, pulling into a long, paved drive. Lights up ahead made a small plane sitting on the runway visible.

"I can't leave without seeing her."

"I'm not giving you a choice, Sawyer. Listen to me; I'll make sure that Vida knows how to find you. You know Vida; what do you think she will do?"

Vida wouldn't stop until she found her, if she knew where she was.

"Colton and she have become close. Do you want to ruin that for her?"

"Where will I go?" Sawyer begrudgingly accepted that King wasn't going to let her get near Vida.

"From what I hear, Vida wasn't the only one to find someone." Sawyer blushed when she realized he was talking about Kaden.

"I don't know if he even wants me back." The last she had seen him, he had been talking with Tatiana. Maybe they had worked things out and she would be in the way. She didn't want to see him with another woman.

"I think that's a question you have to ask him," King stated. "But either way, he'll see you're safe until this mess is finished. Digger has to be more cautious away from Queen City. He has half the police force in his pocket here."

"How do you know?"

"Because I have the other half," he admitted.

The man in the front seat got out of the car after talking briefly on the phone, coming to stand outside her door. "The plane's ready to take off."

Sawyer reached for the door handle, but King reached out to stop her.

Sawyer turned back to him.

"Did you tell him what he wanted to know?" His pitiless eyes stared into hers.

"No."

He tilted his head in curiosity. "Why? From my sources, I heard they were hard on you. Why didn't you tell Digger what he wanted?"

Sawyer broached the subject cautiously. Digger was crazy and mean as hell, but King was the more most dangerous of the two. If King had wanted her, he would have succeeded where Digger had failed. "Because that child deserved to rest in peace."

King paled at her harsh words, his hand dropping away; however, years of holding in her pain had her unable to hold back now.

"No one, not one adult in that building or neighborhood stepped up and stopped Brenda. My mom and Vida's both tried, but she threatened them. Brenda told them that she would disappear with Callie." Tears long held back escaped. "She was so beautiful, King. How could you leave her to that evil woman?"

King paled even further. Pain that she didn't know the man could feel was hard to miss.

"I saw you every day, watching for her to come outside. She didn't even have a fucking doll." A sob broke free. "She didn't even know what a father was, King, until Vida and I told her. How could you turn your back on your daughter?"

The day that Vida and Callie had almost gotten run over by the speeding car would live with her forever. Marshall, Brenda's new live-in boyfriend had purchased a

153

doll for her. Callie had run into the road after it when the neighborhood punks had thrown it toward the road to torment the girls. Vida and she had both chased after her. Sawyer, to this day, didn't know how she'd had the strength to overcome the girls, pulling them to safety in time.

King had not been far behind them. His terror had let his secret slip. It was the one and only time Sawyer was sure that King had lost control. Vida had sat down on the ground, comforting a crying Callie over the loss of her doll. She had not realized how close to death she'd come. King had stood by Sawyer.

"I owe you and Vida, Sawyer. None of the punks in the neighborhood will bother you again." Tears were in his eyes, and his hands were clenched by his side. Even as a young girl, Sawyer could feel the restraint he'd used to hold himself back. Sawyer had seen that look enough in her mother's eyes to know what it meant. The resemblance easily seen between the two as Sawyer's eyes had gone back and forth between them.

"You're her daddy." Sawyer breathed, scared at the look that came in his eyes at her astonishment.

"If anyone finds out who she is, Sawyer, they'll hurt her. Do you want her hurt because you couldn't keep a secret?"

"N—no."

"Then keep your mouth shut. If anyone finds out, I won't be happy. Vida's mom works for me; do you want her to lose her job?" He had shown no compunction in threatening a child.

N—n—no."

"No one will let your mom babysit for them if I tell them not to. Do you want your mom to lose what money she has?"

"N—n—n—no."

"Then keep your mouth shut. You're the only one who knows, so if it gets out, I will know you talked."

Sawyer nodded her head. "I won't say anything, King. I swear."

"I expect you to keep that promise, Sawyer." He left her and her friends without another word, walking away from his beautiful daughter, not looking back.

"I did what I had to do." Kings words drew her back to the present.

"Yes, you did, and you've had to live with losing her everyday just like Vida and I do."

Sawyer opened the car door, stepping out and hanging onto the door for a few seconds. She was blinded by the tears in her eyes. Blinking, she managed to glance back at the grim-faced man.

"I told Digger everything I knew. I didn't tell him you were her father because you weren't a father to her when she was living, and you sure as hell don't deserve to be called her father when she's in a casket paid for by the state." She slammed the car door in finality.

King's bodyguard escorted her toward the plane with a gun in his hand, while four armed security guards were waiting outside the plane. Damn, King was making sure she got on the plane.

As she drew closer, two of the men came forward to escort her up the steps, the other two following behind.

The plane was opulently decorated. Sawyer was staring around, awestruck. She had never been in an airplane before and this one rivaled the tour bus.

As she walked forward, Alec and Kaden rose from their seats. Sawyer started crying again at his haggard look. He looked pale and as if he had lost weight.

When he reached her, he pulled her into his arms, holding her close.

"Woman, you're never leaving me again."

Chapter Nineteen

The plane landed safely two hours later in Chicago with a car waiting for them at the airport. Kaden hadn't left her side. When they'd arrived back at the bus, he had barely given the others time to greet her before he was maneuvering her towards the bedroom. As soon as the door closed behind them, he was pulling and tugging her clothes off.

Each bruise and mark he exposed felt the brush of his lips. When he had completely undressed her, he carried her to the shower.

"I wish it was a bath," he apologized unnecessarily.

"It's okay."

He removed his own clothes before stepping into the shower where she leaned her head on his chest as he soaped her body.

"I've never felt so frightened, Kaden," she confessed.

"Me, either. I thought they would make you disappear before we could find you." He turned her body so that the water washed the soap away.

From the first time she laid eyes on him, she could tell he had suffered at her disappearance. She enjoyed letting him care for her. The exquisite feeling of being safe in his arms was what she had clung to when Digger had been beating her.

"Sawyer, did he…?"

Sawyer shook her head at his delicate question. "He was too scared to go too far with me. He knew King was barely holding back and there was something else preventing him from going overboard with me as well. I don't know if I could have taken that." Everyone had a breaking point and Sawyer knew herself well enough to be certain that Digger and his men sexually abusing her would have been hers.

"You're a survivor, Sawyer; you've proven that."

"At least those women I was with are free now." Kaden didn't want to upset her; however, those women were only a few among the many whose lives Digger had destroyed.

"I have to get dressed; the concert is in a few minutes. You're going to stay on the bus."

"But I want to stay with you." Sawyer wasn't ready to be away from him.

"I'm done playing around with your safety, Sawyer. I've hired personal security to watch the bus and you while I perform. I'm not even doing promos. I'll go in just before the concert and come back right after, but I'm not letting you off the bus. You need some sleep and there's a doctor waiting to check you out.

"Okay," Sawyer gave in, seeing his worry. If staying on the bus relieved his anxiety, then she could do that.

They dried off, returning to the bedroom where Kaden helped her into a large robe, tying it securely around her waist. She then sat on the edge of the bed as she watched him get dressed.

"K—Kaden…" Her fingers played with the belt of the robe.

Kaden zipped up his jeans. "We'll talk after the show, Sawyer," he said, putting on his shoes and t-shirt as a knock sounded on the door.

"It's time to go, Kaden, and the doctor is getting impatient."

"I'm coming."

Kaden came to stand in front of her. Using the lapels of the robe, he pulled her to her feet. Her head fell back as she stared up at the fire in his eyes. His mouth found hers, reassuring her that he still wanted her while at the same time being gentle enough to show her that he had missed her.

"I'll be back in a few." Sawyer smiled as he left and an older woman with graying hair entered, carrying a bag.

"Mr. Cross wants me to check you out."

Sawyer let the doctor exam her. The tension and adrenalin seemed to rush out of her body with Kaden leaving. She suddenly felt overwhelmingly tired and weak. She answered the doctor's questions through a blur. Then the doctor helped her lay down, covering her with the blankets. Sawyer felt as if she couldn't keep her eyes open. She had wanted to be waiting for Kaden when he came back after the concert. *It was just another wish that wasn't going to come true*, she thought as she lost her battle for staying awake.

She barely noticed when Kaden slipped into bed with her since she was unable to even open her eyes. After his hands circled her waist, lifting her to lie across his chest, she felt his hands running soothingly through her hair as she dozed back off. It was the first time she had been able to slip into a deep sleep in his arms.

* * *

"I am not staying on this bus one more day, Kaden." Sawyer crossed her arms over her chest. She had to admit that it would be more effective if she wasn't holding a spatula, but she didn't freaking care. Turning back to the stove, she expertly flipped the burgers she was frying.

"You're not leaving the bus," Kaden replied stubbornly. Sawyer looked at the other band members for help and saw they each were in agreement with Kaden.

Her voice lowered; however, it was just as firm. "If I have to stay locked up another day, I'll go crazy."

Kaden sighed, coming up behind her and wrapping her in his arms. "Sawyer, you scared all of us disappearing like that. None of us ever felt so helpless."

"I know." When she had come out of the bedroom the next day, they had all surrounded her, giving her hugs and letting her know they were glad she was back. Sawyer knew it was silly, but she was beginning to feel a part of them.

"We can all keep an eye on her, Kaden." Sawyer turned in surprise at Sin's voice. She gave him bright smile.

"She can even stand by the curtain the whole show," D-mon added.

"I give in, but no one is allowed into the VIP room before or after the concert." Sawyer expected the others to protest, but they all remained silent in agreement. That was when she knew she wasn't going to be able to leave these men without a hole in her heart for each one.

"I don't agree; I think she should stay on the bus. We're off for three days before we have to head to our next concert. We could take her out for a few hours tomorrow without worrying about trying to manage the crowd." Ax's voice dimmed her enthusiasm.

Kaden looked like he was about to change his mind, therefore Sawyer quickly pleaded her case before he could. "Please, Kaden. I'll be good. I promise I'll stay next to Alec the whole time. If you remember, I wasn't kidnapped from the arena, it was the bus." Sawyer gave him the same smile she had perfected to win her mother when she wanted to do something that her mother didn't think was safe.

"All right. Sawyer, you can go, but if anything goes wrong..." His expression left no doubt of the repercussions if she misbehaved.

"I will." Her happiness shone in her expression.

She made each of the burgers for the men their own individual way she knew they liked them in reward. Except for Ax, his was a little burnt and she deliberately forgot he hated cheese.

She was excited about getting off the bus. She couldn't explain why, though. It basically was switching one confining space for another, yet it was the freedom to move around that she appreciated. The band had recognized that need.

Later that day, as she dressed for the show, she went to the closet to pull out something different to wear, wanting to please Kaden. The four days she had been back, he hadn't touched her intimately, nor had they had the talk he'd promised. She was becoming increasingly concerned that he had decided to renew his relationship with Tatiana, but she was waiting until the danger with Digger was settled before she brought it up.

Kaden had turned R.J. over to the police for assisting in her kidnapping. She had disliked the man ever since she had first met him, but R.J. was seriously whacked in his obsession to put the band back together. Alec had even investigated Jesse's crash and discovered that his brakes had been tampered with. Kaden believed that R.J. had caused the accident to force Kaden out of retirement.

She pulled on a pair of expensive jeans that were just as faded as her cheap ones and a t-shirt that was smaller than she usually wore, showing the swell of her breasts. Opening several shoeboxes, she searched for what she was looking for until she found a tiny pair of filigree sandals with flowers weaved across the back. They gave her a couple of inches in height as well as giving her the feeling of being sexy when she walked. Going into the bathroom, she opened the cosmetic case, took one look and closed it, deciding to take one step at a time.

She brushed out her hair, pulling it back at the top and sides to give it some lift. Stepping back, she took a long look at herself before opening the cosmetic case once again and pulling out a candy pink lip gloss.

Tearing open the new lip gloss, she applied a light amount. Her face was still bruised so she applied a light concealer as well. Feeling better that Kaden wouldn't be accused of abuse, she closed the case and went back into the bedroom. She saw that he was dressed and waiting for her with a worried frown on his forehead.

"It will be fine, Kaden. You worry too much," Sawyer said, coming to a standstill. "Is something wrong?" Kaden shook his head.

"We have six more concerts to get through then we can disappear."

"We?" Sawyer broached the tender subject. Kaden stiffened.

"You have other plans?"

"I can't just disappear without Vida, Kaden. We've had plans since we were little girls." Kaden stood stiffly before going to the door, placing his hand on the knob. "King told me she's found someone, Kaden, like I found you, but I can't disappear without telling her first and giving her the option of joining us. I can't lose her, too. She's like a sister to me."

"You plan on her joining us?" His voice was tight.

"Of course, unless you don't want me anymore. I don't want to pressure you. I know you and Tatiana talked…"

"Sawyer, Tatiana and I were over years ago when she went to help me clean my mother's house and tried on one of my sister's dresses. I threw her out of the house and haven't talked to her until R.J. pulled his fucked up stunt."

Sawyer walked across the floor, wrapping her arms around his waist.

A knock on the door sounded. "It's time, Kaden." Alec's timing couldn't have been worse.

Kaden made no attempt to open the door as his arms tightened around her.

"Let's go. Everything will be fine. You'll see. It'll be boring, everything will go so well."

She laughed at his dubious expression. "How wild could it be in Indiana?"

Chapter Twenty

Sawyer stood in the shadows as she listened to Kaden's song. The audience loved him. There were thousands of singers, but unless they had the charisma to pull the audience into the song, then the music could never reach its potential.

Kaden was one of those vocalists who could sing anything and compel the audience into a realm he controlled with his voice, making you feel each song as if he'd written and sung it just for you.

"He's special, isn't he?" Sawyer whispered to Alec.

"Yes, he is. Last time, he let his fame control him. Now, he controls it. It's taken a long time, but this time, I think Kaden can survive this world."

"You remained friends after you both left rehab?" Sawyer had wondered about his relationship with Kaden.

"Yes. Kaden, Ax and I would spend weekends together, about once every month or two." Sawyer studied Alec, seeing the lines around the eyes of a man much older.

"Boys' night out? Fishing? Gambling?" she teased.

"We like to go to a particular club where we have a

membership. It's a private club where we can express our passions with others." Sawyer's attention jerked from Kaden to Alec.

"P—p—passions?" she asked tentatively.

"Yes, Sawyer. Passions. I have a particular passion for bondage and dominance."

"And K—K—Kaden?"

"Kaden's is dominance and submission, but you already know that, don't you, Sawyer?" The serious expression on his face reminded her of the time he'd waited outside the shop where Kaden had taken her to buy her paddle. She swallowed hard. She wasn't going to ask about Ax.

"Ax's passion is the same as mine." Her eyes went to Ax playing the guitar. She had thought he was the easiest going of the band members.

Sawyer decided that was where her nosiness ended. It was none of her business what Kaden, Ax and Alec had done in the past. She had known Kaden was dominant; however, the extent he lived the lifestyle was a shock, as were his friends' involvement. It should be Kaden who decided when and what to tell her, though.

"No questions?"

"Nope." Her eyes returned to the stage. "You know something, Alec? Every concert I watch Kaden dance with Alyce and whatever women he lets on the stage with him, yet I haven't danced with him, not once." Alyce rubbed her ass up against Kaden's leather pants, her ass grinding back on his cock. Laughing, she twirled her head, smiling at Sawyer watching from the side of the stage.

"I don't care how you live your life. I don't care that Kaden will probably be with another woman in six months. I don't want to think of any of that tonight. Tonight, I just want to be happy that I'm off that bus, and that, when we leave here tonight, that bitch will be going to another bus. If I can survive being kidnapped by Digger twice, I can certainly handle what you're trying to warn me about." Sawyer reached to her side, taking his hand in hers and giving it a squeeze.

Alec returned her tight squeeze. "Kaden's a lucky man."

"I'll tell him you said so," Sawyer laughed.

"I'll tell him myself," he said gruffly.

The crowd parted at the front of the stage where several men dressed in similar leather jackets were working themselves forward, closer to the stage. Sawyer's eyes studied them. They weren't Kaden's usual fans, being older and rougher looking. One scared her just from the scar on his face. The other man was just as large as King's man, which was freaking huge. The closer she studied the men and the crowd, the more she saw that several were wearing motorcycle jackets. She took a step forward, trying to read the name emblazed on their jackets, but Alec pulled her back.

"I've been keeping an eye on them since they came in about fifteen minutes ago." Grimly, he put her further up against the wall so that she was hidden in the shadows.

"They're probably just here for the music." It was weird, yet none of the men were watching the stage, all their attention felt trained on her.

"Yeah, and I plan on going to mass tonight." Alec spoke into his earpiece, telling his men to move in closer.

Sawyer's eyes searched the crowd until her attention was caught and held. He also wasn't paying attention to what was going on with Kaden and the band. He pinned her in place with cold eyes that were expressionless.

"Let's move. Kaden said he wants you back on the bus." Alec took her arm in a firm grip.

"He can't say anything; he's on the stage." Kaden hand signaled again and this time Sawyer caught it. She was about to follow Alec when the crowd swelled, surging forward and coming too close to the stage and overturning a barrier placed to the side. The out of control fans prevented them from exiting.

All hell broke loose as Alec tried to move her backwards to the only other exit across the stage. The crowd had swelled and overwhelmed the security he had in place within seconds. The band stopped playing and tried to get off the stage, but were trapped. It was a flash mob that had gone out of control.

Sawyer felt Alec's hand on her arm go limp suddenly as one of the men hit him in the head with a small club. Two others grabbed her arms, pushing her into the crowd.

"Kaden!" she screamed.

Kaden and the band were desperately fighting their way toward her; however, the forward momentum of the crowd slowed them down. Sawyer fought the men who were dragging her from the stage; they were using the crowd to hide her abduction. Her efforts were useless; she was moved unrelentingly further into the crowd.

An elbow found the face of one of her abductors, sending him careening away. Several others were peeled away as an arm went around her waist, lifting her up off the floor and holding her steady. Her other abductor disappeared into the crowd. The huge man wearing the motorcycle jacket was holding her steady, using his body as a barricade.

Sawyer searched for Kaden and found him fighting through the crowd toward her, D-mon and Sin by his side. Ax, she saw, was helping Alec to his feet. The men in the motorcycle jackets were helping the security guards regain control, forming a line and steadily pushing the crowd backwards.

The large man holding her up didn't budge against the crowd. Sawyer placed her arm around his shoulder to steady herself. She blinked at him when his fist flashed out, popping one of the crowd members like in the whack-a-mole game and the aggressive fan went down. Another tried to move past him and he took them down by the same method. He grinned at her, and Sawyer saw he was enjoying himself, trying to see how many he could knock out.

"Um, uh… I think they're trying to get away."

"I know." Sawyer stifled her laughter as he took out two more. Kaden barely was able to jerk back in time to miss being taken out.

"Stop, he's with me." Sawyer tried to wiggle away from the man holding her, but his grip didn't loosen.

"Let her go."

"I think I'll keep her a little while longer until this crowd thins out a little more." The man refused to release her, so Kaden stepped forward.

"Stop, Kaden." Sawyer stopped him. She wasn't being hurt and she didn't want Kaden to end up in the pile at their feet.

"You can let her go now, Max." Sawyer twisted in the man's arms, startled that his arm was braced under her ass. The man addressing the one holding her was the blond man who had been staring at her before the riot.

"What's the hurry, Ice?" Max handed her to Kaden who held her against him, her feet still not touching the floor. Sawyer glared up at Kaden who refused to set her down.

"Thanks for your help," Kaden spoke up as security finally regained control, shoving the crowd out the doors. Sin, D-mon and Ax came to stand by Kaden.

Ice didn't seem impressed with the band staring at him threateningly.

"No problem. Call it a favor for a mutual friend." His cold gaze watched her reaction.

"Who's the friend?" Kaden asked.

"Vida."

This time Sawyer succeeded in twisting free. "You know Vida?" Sawyer asked eagerly.

"Sawyer," Kaden said, hooking an arm around her waist and pulling her back.

"She belongs to one of my brothers," Ice answered

"Is she here?" Sawyer craned her neck, trying to spot

her friend.

"Fuck, no. Colton wouldn't let her budge her ass out of the hotel room." This time Ice's gaze went to Kaden's, his tone implying that Kaden hadn't taken Sawyer's safety as seriously.

"I want to see her." Sawyer couldn't wait to see Vida.

"Tomorrow. Jackal will call your security chief and set up a meet," Ice spoke to Kaden, ignoring Sawyer's demand.

"I want to see her tonight," Sawyer repeated.

"You will meet Vida when and where we say." Ice and his men began to move away.

Sawyer went to go after them, but was still held tightly by Kaden.

"Sawyer."

"Let me go, Kaden. They have to—"

"Sawyer." This time the fury in his voice had her going still in his hold. "Did you pack the paddle?."

Chapter Twenty-one

Sawyer slowly walked beside a still angry Kaden toward the waiting limo. The usually mild-mannered Ax was tight lipped as he and the other group members followed behind.

Kaden opened the limo door, moving aside so that Sawyer could slide in. Before any of the others could climb in, his arm blocked the door.

"Alec, how long is the ride to the hotel?"

"Thirty minutes."

Sawyer crossed her arms over her chest. It was going to be a long ride to have to listen to Kaden's recriminations.

"Sin and D-mon, ride with Alec." Kaden removed his arm, allowing Ax to climb inside while neither of the other men protested leaving with Alec.

Sawyer didn't say a word as Kaden slid in next to her.

When the limo started pulling away from the arena, Sawyer looked forward to the dark glass that hid the driver from view, and didn't meet Ax's eyes who sat on the seat across from her.

"I don't know why you're so angry with me. It's not my fault that—"

"Be quiet, Sawyer." Kaden's angry gaze shifted to her, making her swallow the rest of the sentence she had been about to say.

She watched as he took a deep breath, relaxing back against the seat.

"Sawyer, I have come to the conclusion that I have been too lenient with you. You don't take your personal safety seriously. For a woman who has been kidnapped twice and has been repeatedly reminded by Alec and myself that you are still in danger, your laissez faire attitude is fucking stupid."

"Laissez faire?" Sawyer questioned.

Kaden's jaw tightened. "Not helping us keep you safe."

"I know what you meant. I'm not a dumb ass. I just meant that I do take my safety seriously, Kaden," Sawyer unwisely snapped back.

"I blame myself. I let myself fall victim to your deliberate wiles, which I can only think have been perfected from years of practice."

"I don't have any wiles. You've got to be freaking kidding me, Kaden." Sawyer refused to acknowledge that she might have given him a smile that would work on her mother occasionally. Besides, he was a grown ass man; she hadn't twisted his arm.

"No, I'm not kidding. I'm beginning to think that, like all children, most of your resentment toward your mother came from the times you weren't able to manipulate her into giving into your spoilt demands."

Sawyer was so angry her mouth opened and closed without a word coming out.

"Close your mouth, Sawyer. Now, I did warn you that there would be consequences if there was any trouble at tonight's concert, didn't I?"

"Yes." This time she could have sworn she heard his teeth grind together at her sarcastic reply.

"Since Ax was the only one to see through your wiles, I thought he deserved a reward and an apology from you."

"What?" Sawyer's mind flew, not understanding just what Kaden was saying. Before she could ask, Kaden's order had her stiffening in her seat.

"Take off your top, Sawyer."

Her eyes flew to Ax's unsympathetic gaze staring back at her.

"Now, Sawyer, or you're going to make it much worse for yourself."

Sawyer's hands went to the bottom of her t-shirt, slowly pulling it off. She sat on the seat with her white bra and jeans.

"Take off your bra."

Sawyer's defiance fled with his order. It was finally sinking in just how angry Kaden was with her.

Her hands went to the front snap of her bra, unsnapping it with trembling fingers. Ax's gaze swept over her firm breasts, each with a tiny nipple ring.

"Have they healed?" Ax questioned Kaden.

"Are they still sore?" Kaden asked her, reaching out to flick one of the tiny rings.

"N—n—no."

"Good." Ax's detached smile had her stomach doing flip flops.

Kaden's mouth went to her breast, teasing the nipples that had been pierced before her kidnapping.

She tensed in his arms as his tongue played with the rings, hardening her nipples and sending sensations of need to her pussy. Her thighs clenched together as Kaden's hand went to her jeans, unsnapping them then sliding the zipper down.

The small bite of pain as Kaden played with her nipple rings increased her arousal. When he reached to slide down her jeans, she willingly lifted her hips. It was only as he sat back that she remembered that they had an audience. She went to pull her jeans back up, but Kaden stopped her, expertly lifting her wiggling body and placing her on his lap to remove her sandals with a flick of his wrist before he then finished removing her jeans.

"Kaden." Her hands went to his chest, unable to believe how quickly he had undressed her in the limo. Her bare ass was sitting on his lap, and she was able to feel the bulge of his cock through his jeans.

"Since I warned you of the consequences, I will give you my punishment first. Considering that Ax was right that you should have stayed on the bus and received an inedible hamburger for his concern, he will give his punishment next."

Before Sawyer could react, she found herself tossed over Kaden's lap with her head and shoulders hung down towards the floorboards. The first smack of his bare hand on her ass had her reaching back to cover her pained posterior.

"Position, Sawyer. Move your hand again and you'll get twice the punishment."

His hand landed on her ass four more times—two on each cheek. When he'd finished, his hand rubbed the pinking flesh before one finger slid through the cleft of her pussy, seeking and finding the betraying wetness. He stroked her clit until a moan escaped her lips.

Gently, he rose her back up into a sitting position.

"Sawyer." Kaden's unforgiving voice reminded her quickly what he required of her.

"I'm sorry, Kaden. The next time I won't argue with you about my safety."

"Good girl." He nodded to Ax who slid into the seat next to Kaden and flipped her over his own lap.

"W—what... w—wait." Sawyer's legs kicked out, trying to stop the embarrassing spanking.

Ax's hand landed on her ass harder than Kaden's. "Ouch. That hurts, Ax." His hand landed even harder.

"Quiet, Sawyer. I can see that you have wrapped Kaden around your finger. That stops now. Do you understand me?"

"Y—yes." His hand landed another swat on her ass.

"Have you given her a safe word?" Ax asked Kaden.

"No, frankly I haven't pushed her hard enough to need one." Sawyer heard the amusement in Kaden's voice.

"I can see that from her behavior. Sawyer, do you know what a safe word is?"

"Yes," her mumbled reply could barely be heard.

"Good. So there is no misunderstandings, I will make it simple for you. Green is go." Sawyer felt his finger slip between her thighs, sliding in her wetness and spreading it towards her clit, giving the tiny bud a brief stroke before removing his hand. "Yellow means you're okay, but don't go any further." his hand went to her breast, slightly tugging on her nipple ring. "Red means stop immediately." His hand returned to her ass.

"Do you understand?"

"Y—yes."

"Good. Now let's finish your punishment." His hand rose and landed against her ass again.

"Red!" Sawyer wailed.

Sawyer heard both assholes' laughter. "Of course I will take into consideration that you're trying to get out of a well-deserved punishment." He administered two more hard smacks to her rear before he raised her and instead of placing her back on Kaden's lap, placed her on his own. This time it was Ax's hard cock pressing against her sore butt.

"Now, what do you have to say for yourself?"

Sawyer rapidly blinked away the tears filling her eyes. "I'm sorry. I shouldn't have ignored your concern." Seeing his unrelenting look, she continued, "I shouldn't have made you a bad lunch because I was angry at you."

"I accept your apology. Now, what is the correct way you thank Kaden for your punishment."

Sawyer's eyes lifted to Kaden's, seeing from the desire flaming in his eyes that watching Ax spank her had excited him. Sawyer couldn't believe what she was about to do next. She leaned over and unzipped Kaden's jeans before pulling his hard cock out. She lowered her mouth to the swollen head of his dick, sucking it into the warmth of her mouth. His hand went to her hair, pushing her head down further on him.

"Suck me harder," Kaden groaned, adjusting his hips until he could thrust easily into her mouth.

Sawyer felt Ax playing with her nipple rings, pulling and tugging on them until they became sensitive to each of his movements. One of his hands slid between her thighs, brushing against her clit before spearing her with a long finger. With Ax's movements heightening her desire, she began sucking more greedily on Kaden's cock, realizing the situation had long since gone out of her control.

Ax slid another finger deep inside then began a steady pumping that mirrored her movements on Kaden's cock. With a deep groan, Kaden released his climax, holding her head in place with her hair until he finished.

When he removed his hand, Sawyer raised her head at the same time that Ax's fingers slid from her pussy, leaving her hanging on the precipice of her climax. With a needy cry, she felt Kaden lift her to his lap. His hand going into her hair and pulling her head back for a tongue thrusting kiss that escalated her needs instead of bringing her down.

"Now, thank Ax for your punishment." Sawyer's eyes went to Kaden's, making sure she had heard him right.

Sawyer was definitely out of her depth, about to use her caution light, but the desire in both men's eyes had her doing the unthinkable. With shaking fingers, she reached out to unbutton Ax's jeans and hesitantly pulled out his cock. The dark plum head made her pause at the size, but her head obediently lowered as Kaden's hand guided her downward.

She sucked Ax's cock into her mouth, feeling her mouth stretch wide to take him. He leaned back, raising his hips to thrust further into her mouth. Kaden maneuvered her body until she was on her knees between the men and her pussy was within reach of his mouth.

Sawyer's mouth slid down further on Ax when Kaden's mouth went to her pussy, finding her opening with his tongue and thrusting it deep before pulling it out, licking her opening and then thrusting it back inside her clenching sheath.

Sawyer wanted to scream at the pleasure and lust taking over her body. The guilt that she had from having sex with two men at the same time—something that went against everything she believed herself capable of—was almost unbearable, yet the experience didn't feel dirty to her. She felt cared and protected by the fact that both men had been deeply upset that she had almost been hurt and abducted. She sought to make it up to them the only way she could; by showing them she understood she had been wrong to place herself in jeopardy.

Ax's fingers squeezed the plump flesh of her breast as he slid his cock in and out of her mouth, barely giving her time to adjust to his size. It took several tries before she could take him comfortably, loosening her throat muscles, and she was rewarded when he groaned, giving her his climax as his hips plunged one final time. Kaden's tongue was replaced with his cock as he lifted her backwards when she raised her head, gasping for breath.

Plunging her down on his cock, Sawyer braced her knees on each side of his hips as she lifted hers, slamming herself down on his thrusting cock. Her back arched at finally having her pussy filled and her hips began grinding herself down on him, trying to reach her own climax.

"Do you want to come, Sawyer?"

"Yes," Sawyer moaned.

"Then give Ax your tit." Sawyer leaned sideways, her hand going to her breast and holding it out to Ax who sucked the tip into his mouth, gently biting down on the nipple ring.

Her movement of leaning towards Ax had Kaden's cock stabbing at a spot within her cunt that sent her into ecstatic spasms. Her screams of release filled the limo as it drew to a stop. Ax's mouth released her now red tipped breast as he leaned back.

"I accept your apology, Sawyer, and look forward to you misbehaving again."

Chapter Twenty-two

Sawyer stood looking out the hotel window, becoming more and more impatient as the day progressed and no one told her when she would be able to see Vida. The men had all disappeared this morning before she woke, and when she had tried to leave the hotel room, Alec had been standing outside her door.

"Where's everyone at?" Sawyer had questioned Alec.

"The band is interviewing new tour managers since they have a three-day layover."

"Oh." Kaden hadn't mentioned that the band would be hiring someone to replace R.J. Did that mean that he would be returning to the band fulltime?

Sawyer shoved her hands into her pockets. "I want to see Vida."

"When the arrangements have been made, you'll be the first to know," Alec replied.

Sawyer started to get angry at his evasiveness; finding herself confined once again didn't help her attitude.

"But I don't want to wait."

"Kaden said that if you started to get difficult for me to call Ax." The amusement shining from his eyes had her biting back her next remark. She went back into the hotel room, slamming the door behind her.

Controlling herself from picking something up and throwing it, Sawyer took deep breaths until she calmed her temper. She spent the rest of the morning on the e-reader Kaden had given her.

After what felt like hours, she was unable to sit still any longer, so Sawyer got up and went to the window, gazing out blindly. When they had arrived at the hotel last night, they each had redressed in the limo before Kaden had unlocked the door. As soon as the driver opened the door, Sawyer had taken off, jumping over Ax before he had time to move out of the way. She almost landed on her head. Only Alec standing nearby had saved her from a nasty fall. He had set her on her feet, searching her face. Her telltale blush had been hard to hide.

His eyes went over her shoulders, giving an imperceptible nod before leading her away. They crowded into the private elevator with D-mon and Sin in a good mood that they had the next three days off, joking with each other. The elevator opened, leading them to two suites. She held her hand out for one of the keys and he didn't hesitate in handing her the key before moving out of the way. She unlocked the door and went inside; about to lock the door behind her until she remembered what had happened the last time she had locked the door.

Searching through the two bedrooms, she found her suitcase had already been sent up. Finding a nightgown, she went into the bathroom and lowered the lid of the toilet where she had sat down to take a few deep breaths. Using her years of speech therapy, she was finally able to get her breathing back under control.

She showered and then slipped on her nightgown before going back into the bedroom. A trolley had been rolled in with several trays, and her empty stomach immediately had drawn her to the appetizing aromas permeating the room.

"Sawyer." Her feet stopped. She hadn't noticed Kaden in the chair in the shadows by the window.

"K—Kaden I—I really don't want to talk to you right n—now."

He stood to his feet, taking her in his arms as her head dropped to his chest.

"I—I can't believe I did those t—things. I—I'm just like those women who let Sin and D-mon—"

Kaden picked her up, carrying her to the chair before sitting down with her on his lap.

"You're nothing like those women, Sawyer. I saw that the first time I stared into your eyes. When you've lived the type of life I've led, you see who's real and who's not.

"You stutter when you get upset, you tug your hair when you're worried, and you're generous and kind. That's why you reacted that way in the limo; not because you take sex lightly. You knew that you'd scared the shit out of both us. You are aware that Ax cares about you. He would steal you from me in a second if he didn't know I would kill him."

Sawyer relaxed against him, unconsciously twirling her hair between her fingers.

"Feel better?"

"Yes. I don't want to kill you anymore. I'll settle for castrating you if it happens again."

"That's an easy fix; just behave, Sawyer. Take your safety as seriously as we do and quit fighting our protecting you. Your friend, Vida, obviously listened to Colton."

"I promise I'll be more careful, Kaden."

* * *

When Sawyer heard the door opening, she turned, expecting Kaden; however, Vida stood in the doorway, grinning at her.

"Vida!"

"Sawyer!"

Both friends ran into each other's arms, crying, and neither could talk for several minutes.

"Thank God, you're safe. I've been so worried about you." Vida looked her friend over carefully before hugging her close again.

"I've missed you so much." Sawyer couldn't stop crying as she stared at Vida, noticing the changes in her. They were as close as sisters and Sawyer saw that the unhappy memories that had always filled her eyes had been replaced with happiness.

They sat down on the couch, still holding each other's hand. It was a habit they'd had since children when her mother would take them for walks in the park, making them hold onto each other's hands. It had been traumatic the first few times they had went to the park after Callie's death, each of them kept unconsciously searching for their missing friend's hand.

"Are you all right?" Vida questioned her, lowering her voice.

Sawyer glanced up, seeing the room of the suite was filled to capacity. Kaden, the band, Alec—with two of his security guards who were wearing FBI vests—Colton—who still looked the same as when he had tattooed her—the bikers—Ice, Max and several others, wearing Predators' jackets.

"I'm fine, but have you counted to see who has the biggest entourage?" Sawyer joked, trying to lighten the atmosphere.

Vida laughed, brushing away her tears. "I don't have to. I do. There's more outside the door and downstairs."

Sawyer smiled gratefully at the men for making sure Vida was safe.

"How did you get away from Rick?" Vida asked.

"Kaden rented me then wouldn't give me back," Sawyer answered, going on to tell her about her second kidnapping and how King had rescued her.

"He must have sent Ashley to warn me. She's the reason I knew how to find you."

"Why didn't he just call and tell you himself?"

"No one has heard from him since the night the FBI raided the recording studio. He might have been afraid the police would arrest him."

Sawyer shook her head. "King is too smart for the police to catch." She ignored the frosty gazes of the FBI agents. "I think he's gone after Digger."

Vida nodded her head in agreement. "I agree. I hope he finds him. Digger is evil and deserves everything that King does to him. He killed a FBI agent that was a friend of mine."

Sawyer didn't tell her that wasn't the worst of the sins that hell was waiting to make Digger pay for. She prayed every night for the women that Digger had kidnapped.

"Sawyer, do you know why Digger wants us?"

"He's trying to find a connection between King and us."

"But there isn't one," Vida protested then, seeing the look in Sawyer's eyes, she asked, "Is there?"

"No, Vida, there's no connection between King and us," then she added softly, "but there was between him and Callie."

"No, Sawyer, there wasn't." Vida stood up, jerking her hand away from her friend.

"King was Callie's father," Sawyer told her.

"No!" Vida started crying and Sawyer joined her. Discussing Callie was bringing back all the heartache they had never been able to leave behind.

"How could he just stand back and not do anything?" Vida cried.

"I don't know, Vida. I really don't. I know she was born during the time of his sister's death. Maybe he thought he was protecting her. Instead, he left her in the hands of pure evil. Brenda makes Digger look like a choirboy. I told Digger about Callie, that she was a friend of ours, but I didn't tell him that King was her father. I told him there wasn't a connection that I knew about. I don't think he believed me, though. His hatred of King has gone too far. He can't back down now without taking King down, and he thinks King would try to save us."

Vida and Sawyer both sat quietly, thinking.

"He would, wouldn't he, Sawyer? He'd sacrifice himself for us."

"Yes. He believes he owes us for saving Callie that day. King always pays his debts," Sawyer answered.

"This is such a mess. What are we going to do now? King and Digger are both missing." Vida and Sawyer stared at each other, unsure of what their next step should be. They'd always had a plan of action since they were kids.

"I can answer that question." Kaden stepped forward, walking to the couch and sitting down beside Sawyer. "We have the hotel secure; you two can stay here until the band has to be at their next concert. Then, you two need to be moved to a safe house."

Sawyer started to protest then remembered her promise about taking her safety more seriously. "Where?"

"I have a remote cabin that you both could stay in with Alec's security guards. As soon as the tour is over, I can join you and we can decide where to go next."

Vida and Sawyer both looked at each other as Colton walked over, sitting down next to Vida. "It's a good idea, Vida. If you go back to Queen City, Digger won't stop. If he's finally made a move toward King, he won't back down until one of them is dead. Digger's operation is exposed; he has nothing to lose."

Sawyer saw Vida's nod of agreement. "Then I guess we're all going to Kaden's cabin."

Looking at Kaden and the band, then at the rough appearance of the Predators, Sawyer thought the next few days were going to be interesting.

Chapter Twenty-three

"Where are you, Kaden? They're holding the plane for you."
Grace's voice sounded worried.

"I'm stuck in a meeting. R.J. is going to get me another plane tomorrow. You guys go ahead." Tatiana motioned to him from where he was standing with R.J. and Briana. R.J. had convinced him to stay overnight and meet his family tomorrow due to the Christmas party he had thrown the band.

"Kaden, you are going to show, aren't you? We miss you. Please, Kaden, it's Christmas."

"I said, I'll be there in the morning." His voice sounded sharp, but he made no effort to soften his tone. *"Put Mom on and I'll tell her myself."*

"Kaden—"

"Grace," he mocked, *"put Mom on."* The rustling of the phone could be heard then his mother's voice came over the line.

"I'm stuck in a meeting. The plane is going to take you guys then come back for me."

Silence was his only answer.

"Mom, I'll be there in the morning before the kids open their presents." Kaden lifted his glass of whiskey for another drink.

"Okay, Kaden. We'll see you in the morning. I love you."

Resignation sounded in her voice.

"I'll be there, Mom. I won't let you down." Kaden knew he was lying, planning on calling in the morning with another excuse.

"I know you won't. I'll see you in the morning." The line disconnected with a final click.

Kaden sat up in the bed, sweat drenching his flesh as he ran his hand through his damp hair.

"Kaden, are you all right?" Sawyer's sleepy voice sounded from the side of the bed. When they had gone to bed, she had been in his arms, but she always managed to slip away from him during the night. She couldn't sleep pinned down by his weight.

"I'm fine; just a bad dream."

The covers rustled as she rolled over closer to him, curling against his side.

"Quit fighting them, Kaden." Her hand reached out, stroking his chest as she pressed him back to the bed.

"Fighting what?"

"The memories."

His arm came up to lay across his eyes, trying to shut out her words.

"You don't understand, Sawyer."

"I understand what it's like to lose someone you love. The pain is so bad that you don't let yourself think about it during the day. The only time their memories can get through is when you're sleeping. It's a wonderful gift."

"It's not a gift. It's a punishment."

"Kaden, it's not a punishment."

"Yes, Sawyer, it is." His arm fell back to his side. "I'm responsible for killing my entire family."

"No, Kaden," Sawyer protested.

"I did. I was supposed to meet them at the airport before the plane took off. R.J. had a Christmas party, though. Tatiana and I had been partying pretty heavily and I let R.J. convince me to let them go ahead. I told them that I would be there when they woke up, but I had no intention of going. I was planning to blow them off again."

"It wasn't the first time?"

"No, R.J. discovered me when I was just fourteen. By the time I was eighteen, he had put the band together and we were becoming well known. My mom, at first, tried to keep control, but R.J. overwhelmed her. Then, when I turned eighteen, there wasn't anything she could do. I sold my soul to R.J. for fame."

"No, you didn't, Kaden. You were just young and misguided."

"Because of me, my mother, sister, her two kids and her husband died. My sister was pregnant."

"That's why you had the vasectomy. To punish yourself."

"I don't deserve to have children. It's because of me that three children lost their lives."

"They wouldn't want you to blame yourself, Kaden, and they would have been glad you weren't on the plane." Sawyer knew that there was nothing she could say that would convince him he wasn't responsible.

"When Vida, Callie and I were kids, we thought we were sisters. We would cry at the end of the day when Goldie and Brenda showed up to take them home. My mom was raised in a wealthy neighborhood. I was three when my dad died and we moved into a big apartment building. I didn't realize it was for low income, nor did I understand the desperation that filled the people's lives that lived there. I just knew I had Vida and Callie.

"Everyone in that apartment building knew that Callie was being abused. Hell, everyone in the neighborhood knew it. But every single damn one of them minded their own business; too afraid of Brenda, or the state. There were several families that had undocumented immigrants living with them or women with boyfriends who weren't supposed to be there. They all watched out for themselves. No one watched out for Callie." Sawyer's eyes stared into his, seeing the pain of losing someone reflected back at

her.

"I should have told someone at school. I should have taken her someplace and hidden her. I should have done something." Her voice broke. "Her mother's boyfriend found Brenda in bed with another man. He killed both of them before setting her apartment on fire, then killed himself. They found Callie dead in an apartment next door. She must have run away before he set the fire. Every single day I think of something I should have done to save her.

"I learned the hardest lesson of my life that day. The same one that you learned when you lost your family. That family always comes first. If you were given the opportunity again, would you have made that flight?"

"God, yes. I would have been there for their birthdays, Thanksgiving, the first day of kindergarten. I would've been there." This time it was Kaden's voice breaking.

"I would have called the police. I would have run away with Callie. I would have killed Brenda. I would have done something. That's what we learned, Kaden; the most painful lessons in life are the ones that hurt the most."

They held each other through the night while Kaden talked about his family and Sawyer talked about her mother and Callie. Eventually, they got out of bed, taking a bath together. Sawyer threw in her last bath bomb. She had saved the overpowering floral-scented one for last, not crazy over the smell.

Kaden made a face, sinking into the tub.

"What?" Sawyer giggled at his expression.

"I have a feeling this is going to be another painful life experience."

"Why?"

"Those bikers are going to think I'm a pussy for smelling like a girl."

* * *

Vida and Sawyer had lunch together in Sawyer's room. Kaden had been able to get Vida and Colton a suite next door. For the other bikers, the hotel found rooms on different floors.

Kaden was still interviewing tour managers, but Colton had joined them. Vida told her how King had let her stay at the strip club for her protection.

"They told me that you were staying there; they didn't tell me you were actually stripping." The bastards hadn't told her that part. Suspiciously, she asked Vida, "What was your stage name?"

"Trouble. I wasn't very good at it, even worse giving lap dances." Sawyer had lived with Vida since her mother had died; she knew what kind of body she had. She would bet the men had loved her. Vida was beautiful in a quiet and unassuming way, but her body was a showgirl's dream with long legs and perky breasts.

She cast Colton a look underneath her lashes. "How did she really do?"

"She did great dancing, but I'm still waiting to judge the lap dancing," he said, giving Vida a sensual smile.

Sawyer laughed at his answer.

She noticed the new tat on Vida's collarbone, the intricate lines of the butterfly drawing her eye. "Are those your initials?" She made out the swirling lines of the C and the D.

"Yes."

Wow, the man didn't believe in wasting time.

Sawyer also noticed the color on the back of her wrist when she lifted her glass to take a drink. She reached out, turning her wrist over to get a better look. It was a piece of art.

"It's beautiful, Colton," Sawyer complimented him.

"Thank you."

"If you get time, will you give me another tattoo? I already know what I want."

"If I can get a machine," Colton said.

Sawyer studied the man, who it was obvious her friend was in love with. He had always been good looking, but age and experience had added a sensual appeal that would be hard for a woman to resist. Sawyer was confident enough to know Vida wouldn't have made it easy for him.

At that moment, Kaden came into the suite, slamming the door. He took a seat at the table and poured himself a cup of coffee.

"I take it the interviews are not going well?" Sawyer questioned.

"They're going fine, if I want another R.J.," Kaden said in disgust.

"I really like Jordan." Sawyer knew Jordan would be thrilled with the job.

"Ms. Jordan is too inexperienced for the job."

"That's what makes her perfect. She's eager to please, enthusiastic, and I damn sure don't see her hiring a pimp for the band."

"I'll think about it," Kaden conceded.

"Does that mean that you're considering going back to singing full-time?" Sawyer asked, twirling her hair.

"No, I just want to leave them in better hands this time. I plan on spending my time writing songs, and occasionally singing, but I have no intention of becoming involved in the constant touring and travel."

Sawyer smiled, relieved. She wasn't fond of touring, but she would have done it to make him happy. She could handle the occasional concert and she wanted to travel, just not to the extent his career would require. She stopped her wayward thoughts. Kaden had never really said he was planning on a future together with her after Digger's capture.

"Something wrong?" Vida questioned. Her friend knew her too well not to recognize that something was bothering her.

"N—n—no." Both Kaden and Vida looked at her skeptically.

Sawyer sought to change the subject. "Do Vida and I have to stay inside for the next two days? We have enough security that we should be able to get out for a little while to do some shopping." Kaden and Colton both nodded their heads in agreement.

"The Predators can watch you while you shop. Digger is smart enough not to try anything when you're surrounded by them."

"Take some of Alec's security, too; they'll have the firepower if Digger does get brave," Kaden added.

Colton lifted a brow, not saying anything. Kaden got his message with a nod of his head.

"Go, you'll probably be safer than Fort Knox."

Vida and Sawyer both got to their feet, anxious to relieve their anxiety over Digger with some retail therapy. Sawyer, already dressed, went to go with Vida as she dressed so they could gossip without the men overhearing.

"Sawyer," Kaden's command had her freezing, turning to face him.

"Did you forget something?"

"No, I have my own money; Vida brought my purse."

"I wasn't talking about money." His eyes stared into her until she blushed, walking back to him and then leaning down to brush his mouth with hers. She started to stand, but his hand on the back of her neck held her captive as he took control, giving her no opportunity to evade his kiss.

"Now you can go," he said, releasing her. The girls had the door open this time when Colton's voice called out.

"Vida." Vida turned back.

"Did you forget something?" His voice mocked Kaden's choice of words.

"Now that you mention it, I did. Come here." Colton grinned as he stood up and walked to Vida's side.

Sawyer's mouth dropped open. He had a lethal sensuality that would make any woman pause. When he stopped in front of Vida, he put his arms around her waist, lifting her against his body and giving her a passionate kiss that had Vida almost losing her balance when he placed her back on her feet. Colton put out a hand to steady her.

Sawyer threw Kaden a dirty look. Obviously she had a thing or two to learn from her younger friend.

Chapter Twenty-four

Sawyer and Vida spent the day shopping. Sawyer was able to replenish her supply of bath bombs, even purchasing several for Vida. Vida picked herself out a few more items of clothing, explaining that Colton and she had left Queen City in a hurry and hadn't brought enough clothes.

The Predators watched them closely, entering the stores with them, making the salesclerks nervous. Sawyer couldn't blame them; their appearance was frightening. She noticed the one with a scar down his cheekbone standing in the store doorway, surveying anyone who entered.

When they stopped for lunch at a small diner, Vida told her all the tricks she had learned about stripping. She couldn't hold back her giggles when she talked about shaking her ass at the crowd as she left the stage.

Sawyer couldn't help it; she laid her head down on the table she was laughing so hard. She had never imagined her shy friend would ever be able to strip, much less shake her ass at a group of horny men.

Suddenly somber, Sawyer took her hand in hers. "I'm so sorry that you went through that, Vida. If I hadn't been stupid enough to go out with Rick, then you wouldn't have had to go to work for King."

"If Rick hadn't kidnapped you, then Briggs or Morgan would have. Digger is determined to find out something to use against King."

"I know. Let's hope the police find Digger, and we won't have to be surrounded by our entourages anymore," Sawyer teased.

"I don't know. I'm beginning to like being surrounded by a large group of men."

"Yours are better looking than mine. Mine look like they have sticks up their asses; yours look like they put them there." Both group of men cast suspicious glances, as if they knew they were the topic of conversation.

When they arrived back at the hotel, the security guards put them on the elevators, radioing Kaden's security that they were on their way up. Sawyer was about to say goodbye to Vida at the door to her room when she got a text message from Kaden, telling her that he was interviewing Jordan, and if she wanted to see her before she left, to come to Jordan's room.

"A woman I met a few weeks ago is here for an interview with Kaden. I'm going to meet them in her room. I'll see you for dinner."

"What about security? Shouldn't you tell them?" Vida stopped her friend, motioning to Alec's security men guarding the elevator.

"Yes, I'll tell them I'm meeting Kaden." Sawyer hugged her friend goodbye before going back to the elevator.

"Kaden just texted me that he's on the tenth floor and I can meet him there."

The security guard talked into his communication device.

"It's okay; security will meet her at the elevator." The guard pushed the button for the tenth floor and the door closed.

Sawyer was happy that Kaden had been thoughtful

enough to let her see Jordan before she left.

Security wasn't waiting outside the elevator. Before she could react, the man she had known as Tommy dragged her from the elevator.

"If you open your fucking mouth, Digger will kill Kaden and that pretty friend of yours."

Sawyer closed her mouth as the man pushed her into a room not far from the elevator. She barely managed to keep her balance, seeing her worst fears confirmed. Alec's two security guards were lying on the carpeted floor, gazing sightlessly up at the hotel ceiling. Sawyer almost began screaming hysterically, but Digger's cruel gaze caught hers. She stifled the screams in her throat. He had Kaden tied to a chair with a gun pointed at his head while Jordan was tied to the bed, unconscious.

A struggle had taken place in the room, which was confirmed by her feet crunching the papers on the floor.

"Watch the door," Digger ordered Tommy.

"D—Digger d—don't do this. Let him g—go."

"I don't give a fuck about this shithead. Where is King?"

"I don't k—know."

Digger moved toward her, raising the gun and hitting her on the side of her face, knocking her to the floor.

Going down to his knees beside her, he jerked her to her feet by her hair.

"I am going to ask you one more time. If you don't tell me the truth, I'll kill the bitch on the bed. What is the connection between you and King?"

"I—I knew who his d—daughter w—was. He felt he owed me and Vida for saving her l—life."

"That other kid who died in that fire?" Sawyer wasn't surprised that he had checked out Callie's death.

"Yes." Sawyer stared at Kaden.

"Damn it. That's useless to me. Where is King?" Digger yelled at her.

"Right here."

They all turned to stare at King standing in the doorway with a gun pointed at Digger. Tommy lay on the floor behind him, and Ax stood behind King.

When King pointed the gun at Digger's head, she knew what he was going to do.

"Don't kill him, King. Please. If you kill him, all those women he's kidnapped will never be found. Can you live with that, too? I know I can't. I still hear their screams. If you ever regretted what happened to Callie, make it up now. Save those women the way you didn't Callie."

King's cold-blooded eyes stared deep into hers before going back to Digger's. A malicious smile spread across his ruthless face right before he fired the gun.

Digger's scream of pain filled the room as his hand that was holding the gun hung uselessly by his side before he fell to the floor.

"You better kill me now, King," Digger said, not raising his head from the floor. "Because I won't stop before I kill you and destroy everything that belongs to you."

"That would be hard to do, Digger. I don't have anything left that I care about," King said, handing the gun he was holding to the FBI agent running in the door.

Sawyer rushed across the floor to Kaden's side, giving a sigh of relief that he was conscious. She untied him with the help of Ax, jumping into his arms when he was released.

"T—thank God, you're okay." His arms pulled her closer.

Sawyer rubbed the blood away from the corner of his mouth.

"Is he okay?" Colton and Vida came to their side, followed by Ax.

"I'm fine," Kaden answered. "How did King find us?"

"Jordan was checking in last night when I was coming through the lobby. I stopped and talked to her for a minute. I remembered her room number when the clerk gave her the key. When Vida checked to make sure that you made it to the room okay and no one answered, we started down here. King had taken care of the guard just as we were arriving," Ax explained.

"Watch out!" Alec yelled.

Everyone turned, seeing Digger had broken away from the paramedic trying to stop the blood, grabbing the gun that lay on the floor, pointing it at Vida. Ax pushed Vida out of the way just as Digger pulled the trigger.

Chapter Twenty-five

"You could stay and finish the tour with us," Sawyer said, wistfully taking Vida's hand in hers.

"We can't. Colton needs to get back to his shop, and I have a couple of job interviews. You could come back with us until Kaden finishes his tour," Vida countered with tears in her eyes.

Kaden's arm around her shoulder stiffened, letting her know that he wasn't happy with that solution. She smiled up at him before taking a step forward, hugging Vida close. "He only has six more concerts then we'll come for a visit," Sawyer promised, subtlety letting Vida know she would be staying with Kaden when she returned to Queen City.

Vida nodded, returning her tight hug. Stepping away, she turned and walked a few feet, coming to stand in front of Ax, whose shoulder and arm were in a sling. Ax looked down at the woman who came to his shoulder.

"You saved my life. I'd hug you, but I don't want to hurt you," Vida thanked him.

"Maybe you can think of another way to pay me back," he joked.

"I'll do that," she said, reaching up to kiss his cheek before going to Colton who sat on his bike, patiently waiting.

The passersby crossed the street to keep from getting near the rough looking bikers. All except Jordan, who was giving Max and the one with the scar on his face, hell for not moving their bikes so that her cab could park. Max was edging his bike forward, out of the way, but the other one was just staring at Jordan like she was a pest to be ignored. It wasn't until Ice spoke that the biker edged forward, finally letting the taxi into the driveway.

Jordan waved goodbye to them as she climbed into the cab, making a different movement of her hand to the biker who had ignored her request.

"Did she just give Jackal the..." Vida laughed, but quieted when all the Predators' glares turned on her.

"She gave him the bird." Sawyer couldn't help but grin at the bubbly girl who hadn't been the least frightened by the large group of bikers. They all watched as the cab pulled out, taking the woman to the airport.

Kaden hadn't made a decision to hire her yet, but she planned on guilt tripping him into it to pay her back for almost getting killed by Digger. To give Jordan credit, she hadn't been too upset; she had been more relieved that the situation had been resolved before she'd regained consciousness.

Vida climbed onto the back of Colton's bike, waving as the large group of bikers pulled out. Kaden's arm returned to her shoulder as he led her onto the bus. Ax and Alec brought up the rear, closing the bus door behind them.

As Sawyer sat down on the chair, looking sadly out the window, Kaden leaned against the kitchen counter, watching Sawyer as the bus pulled out. Her hand was tugging her hair, twirling it around her finger.

Ax sat down on the leather couch groaning.

"You need a pain pill?" Kaden questioned.

"No, thanks; I just took one."

"What are we going to do about tomorrow's concert?" D-mon asked.

"Jesse is flying in tomorrow. He's recovered enough that he can sit on a stool and take Ax's place until he's better. By the end of the tour, both of you can take the next few months off while whoever we decide to hire sets up another tour," Kaden said, pulling out a bottled water from the fridge.

"Sounds good to me." Ax stood up, stretching. "I'm going to go lie down."

They were all grateful their friend was still alive as they watched him go to his compartment, closing the sliding door. It was a horrific moment watching Digger's gun go off. If not for Ax's quick action, there was no doubt that Vida would have been mortally wounded.

Digger was lucky for the second time that day when Alec knocked Digger out instead of killing him. There wasn't a person in the room who didn't want to see the crazy man dead, but they'd all wanted the women he had kidnapped safely returned.

Alec had told them this morning that Digger was under guard at the hospital and that the FBI were waiting to question him.

Sawyer rose, stretching. "I'm going to follow Ax's example and go to bed." Telling everyone goodnight and then reaching up to brush Kaden's mouth with hers, she went into the bedroom and got ready for bed. She lay down on the bed, thinking she would wake up when Kaden came in; instead, she woke up the next morning, wrapped in his arms with him staring down at her drowsy eyes.

"That's the first time that you let me hold you through the night."

"Is it?"

"Yes." His mouth lowered to hers, his tongue slipping into her mouth, and Sawyer's arms slipped around his shoulders as he deepened the kiss.

A knock sounded on the door.

"I have a photo shoot this morning with the local television station."

Her arms dropped to her sides as he levered himself off her. She rolled to her side as she watched him dress.

"I have to go. I'll see you later."

He bent down, giving her a quick kiss before leaving. Sawyer lay in bed several minutes, staring up at the ceiling, before she climbed out of bed and then got dressed. As she pulled out her suitcase, she decided to unpack a few of her clothes since they would be staying on the bus until they finished the tour. Opening the built in drawers, she searched for an empty one. The first few drawers were filled; however, the next had a large envelope in it that was opened. When she started to close the drawer, a photo slipped loose.

Sawyer looked down at the face she recognized. Reaching out, she picked up the thick envelope. She pulled out several pictures of Tatiana that had her nude with Kaden. Sawyer flipped through the pictures, wishing she had never touched the envelope.

Feeling something else in the envelope, she pulled out two cassettes that would fit in a camcorder. When she had heard Kaden tell Alec to get the tapes back, she had assumed he was talking about tapes with songs on it.

She had been a naïve idiot. The pictures in her hand told her that. Carefully sliding the pictures back into the envelope with the two cassette tapes, she closed it before placing it back into the drawer.

Going to her suitcase, she zipped it closed before slipping on her sneakers. Grabbing her purse and suitcase, hoping like hell all the men would be at the interview with Kaden, she stuck her head out of the bedroom door. Seeing no one on the bus, she slipped out of the room. She was passing the bathroom door when the door opened and Ax came out dressed in his jeans.

His eyes fell immediately to the suitcase and purse in

her hand.

"Where are you going?"

"I'm leaving. There's no need for me to be here any longer now that Digger is in custody. Goodbye, Ax." Sawyer kept walking, but was brought to a standstill when Ax's hand jerked her to a stop.

"What's with the attitude? I go to bed last night and everything is cool. I wake up and you're sneaking out of the fucking bus. You get in a fight last night with Kaden?"

Sawyer refused to answer, attempting to jerk away. "I'm leaving, Ax. Let me go."

"What the hell!" He pulled her backward, shoving her back into the bedroom and locking her inside.

"Let me go!" Sawyer yelled, banging on the door.

Silence from the other side of the door was her only answer.

She paced back and forth across the carpeted floor, looking at the clock on the nightstand every few minutes. It was an hour later that the bedroom door was unlocked and a grim Kaden came into the bedroom, staring at her silently.

Sawyer stood, staring back at him angrily. She wanted to throw something at him; she was so hurt.

"Explain yourself, Sawyer."

"I'm done explaining myself to you. I want to leave and I want to leave now!"

"Watch your tone of voice with me or you're going to be sorry. I'm trying to be understanding because I can see you're upset over something, but you're straining my patience with your sarcasm."

"Deal with it, Kaden, or don't, but I'm leaving." Picking up her suitcase was a bad move because Kaden took it from her, throwing it across the room, just before she found herself being lifted and carried to the bed. Expecting to be put over his lap, thinking she would never forgive him, he instead sat down with her on his lap.

"Tell me what's wrong. Couples talk their problems

through. They don't run."

"We're not a couple anymore," Sawyer snapped back.

"Sawyer, you're about five seconds away from an extremely painful life experience if you don't explain what has you so angry."

Sawyer's lips tightened then her ginger broke through. "I found the pictures of you and Tatiana." Her expression revealed her revulsion.

"You went through my things?" Whoa. How did this get turned around on her; she was the one that was angry.

"I didn't mean to. I was looking for a drawer and one of the pictures slid out," Sawyer explained.

"Did all the pictures fall out?"

Damn it, Sawyer thought.

"No."

"Those pictures were taken six years ago. You're going to be angry for something I did six years ago?"

"Yes—no. You're trying to confuse me," she said, frustrated at his refusal to see that he was the one in the wrong.

"I'm not trying to confuse you. I have news for you, Sawyer; I wasn't a virgin when I met you. I've led a very active sex life. In fact, there's not much I haven't done."

"From those pictures, I know there's nothing you haven't done," Sawyer snapped, jerking off his lap. She went to the drawer, taking the envelope out. She opened it and dumped the photos on the bed.

Sawyer pointed at one. "I wasn't the first one you talked into getting her nipples pierced, was I?" She was hurt and angry at herself. She had felt special because she had wanted to have them pierced to please him. When she looked at the picture with Tatiana, it didn't feel special to her anymore.

Kaden reached out, pulling her stiff body between his thighs.

"Tatiana's nipples had been pierced before I even started dating her. A couple of women I've been in sexual relationships with have them, plus a variety of other piercings. Some have had their tongue or lips pierced. A couple their pussies. I didn't try to talk you into those, did I?"

"No," she admitted reluctantly. Damn, she wasn't ready to be talked out of her madness.

"Sawyer, there is no comparison between you and Tatiana."

"I—I know." Her lip trembled.

Kaden's hand splayed the pictures onto the bed. "Look at my face."

Sawyer looked at the photos on the bed, this time looking at his face. The Kaden in those pictures was not the one in this room with her. The Kaden in the picture's face was filled with lust. He was also obviously drugged, the photo catching the glazed look in his eyes. The man in those pictures didn't look at Tatiana the way he looked at her when he made love to her. Sawyer felt a lump in her throat. The way he was staring at her now. The Kaden in the photos had died with his family.

"I'm sorry." Her arms went around his shoulders, her mouth going to his. "I'm so sorry." Kaden's arms pulled her back onto his lap.

"I love you, Sawyer."

"I love you, too, Kaden."

"I have to get back to the interviews. They all probably think I'm back into drugs again the way I took off."

"Go ahead. I'll see you later." His hand cupped her jaw, bringing her eyes to his. "You can destroy those pictures and tapes if you get bored," he said, standing up.

Going to the door, he was about to open it, but he turned back.

"Oh, and Sawyer, you will be punished tonight." He raised a finger for each of her offenses. "You were rude to Ax when he asked where you were going. You were very rude to me when I asked. You went through my personal items, but the one that will really hurt and the one you will never forget, is that you were going to leave without talking to me first."

Kaden then opened the door and closed it behind him.

Chapter Twenty-six

My love for you consumes me, drowns me.
Baby, why can't you see, you're mine for eternity.
Like a bird in a cage with nowhere to go,
These tainted hands hold your soul.

I will make you love me, crave me.
Baby, just you wait and see. I will become your disease.
Like a bird in a cage with nowhere to go,
These tainted hands hold your soul.

You flew away. You didn't stay.
Baby, why didn't I see, you could be stolen from me.
I'm like a bird in a cage with nowhere to go,
These tainted hands need your soul.

You came back. My heart was black.
Baby, look and see. You have finally rescued me.
Like a bird in a cage with nowhere to go,
These tainted hands won your soul.

Sawyer watched Kaden sing from backstage with Alec

standing next to her. Kaden had his shirt off and was wearing leather pants that hung low on his hips. The music was erotic as hell and was thrumming through her body. The sultry lyrics combined with his voice had the audience swaying, holding lights in their hands. The song was moving with an emotional depth that she hadn't heard before.

"Is it a new song? I haven't heard it before." Sawyer turned, asking Ax who was standing behind her.

"Yeah, he started writing it when you were missing. He just finished it a couple of days ago," Ax answered.

Sawyer looked back at the stage, seeing Kaden's eyes were on her. She gave him a sweet smile, loving the song and the man who'd written the lyrics.

When the song ended, another began. Sawyer should have known the touching moment couldn't last. The familiar chords of the song started as Alyce strutted out onto the stage. Kaden and her sang, walking back and forth across the stage. When it came time to do their usual bump and grind on the middle of the stage, Kaden made a turn, walking back to the side of the stage toward her. When he didn't stop, but took her hand and led her out onto the stage, she tried to pull away, embarrassed with the arena's eyes on her. Alyce looked furious; however, she moved to the right of the stage and kept singing while Kaden moved them toward the center before coming to a stop.

Sawyer was frozen stiff at being the focus of attention. She turned to flee the stage, but Kaden's arm went around her waist, holding her in place. Her eyes flew wildly to his, scared to death. She had been kidnapped twice, been beaten by Digger, had bullets shot around her twice, yet standing on stage terrified her.

"Dance with me." The look in Kaden's eyes had her struggles slowing as Kaden's movements against her began to cross the barrier of her stage fright. His hands went to her hips as he continued to sing into his headset.

She gradually relaxed against him, forcing herself to look only at him as she began to move against him. The music she had watched him dance numerous times to with Alyce was easy to move to; however, she couldn't let herself go to the extent that Alyce did. When the song ended, he let her flee the stage back to Alec and Ax's side, who were laughing at her like goons.

"I—I'm g—going t—to k—k—kill h—him." Her comment only made them laugh louder at the same time that Ax's good arm went around her shoulder, drawing her to his side.

After the show, they returned to the VIP room. Kaden had gone to the airport that afternoon to meet Jesse's plane. Then, before the show, the promoters had kept them busy, so it was the first opportunity she'd had to meet Jesse. He was good looking and sexy, but in her eyes, he paled in comparison to Kaden.

Several of the women fans were overwhelmed backstage, unable to restrain themselves and had to be shown out by Alec.

Sawyer sat on one of the couches, watching as Sin, D-mon and Jesse ushered one star struck fan into the restroom. Sawyer could only imagine how wild the group had been when they were younger, if they were like this now that they were older. They showed no signs of slowing down, either.

Ax took a seat next to her on the couch, wincing as he jarred his shoulder.

Sawyer got up, going to get him a beer before bringing it back to him.

"Thanks," he said with a pained smile.

"You're welcome."

"You and Kaden kiss and make up?"

"Yes, we're okay."

"That's good. I don't think he would make it losing another person he loves, Sawyer."

Sawyer lowered her head, feeling guilty that she would

have walked out on Kaden with no explanation.

"I have a little bit of a temper," Sawyer confessed.

Ax shook his head at her ruefully. "I think Kaden will help you get it under control. It's a good thing for you that we're spending the night on the bus and don't have any privacy, but Kaden's promised me a weekend visit when you two find a home. You really shouldn't have been so rude to me this morning when I asked where you were going. I had to take another pain pill after I locked you up." His twinkling eyes promised retribution. Her body clenched and her nipples pebbled under her shirt.

Kaden sat down next to her, his hand pressing down on her thigh, preventing her from getting up from the couch.

"Behave, Ax. I can't tell if you're scaring her or turning her on," Kaden said, searching Sawyer's red face.

"Both," Ax answered for her. Both men sat on the couch with her, talking about the show. Kaden was letting Jesse handle the press and promoters.

Later, Alec escorted them through the remaining crowd as they left the arena back onto the bus. The men were tired but pumped, throwing themselves down on the chairs and couches and pulling out the liquor bottles. Sawyer knew when it was time to retreat.

She went into the bedroom, preparing for bed. She was about to take a shower when Kaden walked in, closing and locking the door behind him.

His eyes took in the nightgown in her hand.

"You're not going to need that tonight, Sawyer." Sawyer paused, looking at his hard face. "Take off your clothes and prepare yourself while I take my shower." She swallowed hard, aware he was not going to let her get away with her behavior from earlier today.

Kaden went into the bathroom, closing the door behind him. Sawyer hurriedly undressed, making sure she folded her clothes and put them away. The running shower shut off and a squeak escaped Sawyer as she barely remembered to lay the paddle on the bed before she took the position Kaden expected to find her in.

She was leaning over the bed with her ass stuck out and her hands on the bed overlapping each other when Kaden opened the bathroom door a second later.

"I see you remembered the paddle." His hand reached out and picked it up. "Tell me something, Sawyer; did you even consider how I would feel when you tried to leave this morning."

"No." The truth got her a hard swat on her bottom.

"No, what?" Another swat.

"No, Kaden."

His fingers went between her thighs.

"That's better." He stroked her clit until her hips thrust back at him.

A firm swat on her ass had her back in position.

"This is for disrespecting Ax." Swat.

"Disrespecting me when I asked what was wrong." Swat, swat, swat, swat, swat.

"Going through my things." Swat.

His hand rubbed the pinking flesh of her butt before going once again to the gathering wetness that gave her excitement away.

"Which one did I tell you would hurt the most?"

"I was going to leave without talking to you first." The hard swat on her bottom had her standing on her tiptoes, but she didn't break position. Sawyer heard him lay the paddle on the nightstand.

"I'm ready to accept your apology, Sawyer."

Sawyer obediently went to her knees on the carpet before him. His naked body gleamed in the light of the bedroom.

"May I touch you, Kaden?"

"Yes."

He groaned when she reached out, taking his hardening cock deep into her mouth. She scooted closer to him on her knees as she began to suck on his dick. Her tongue explored his length as her hand reached out to cup his heavy balls.

His hips thrust forward, driving more of his length inside her warm mouth. Kaden put his hand in her hair, holding her head still as he fucked her mouth. Sawyer whimpered as her pussy clenched, wanting his cock inside her.

Pulling his cock away, he took a step back. "Get on the bed, Sawyer."

Sawyer eagerly went to the bed, thrilled he wasn't going to extend her punishment by not letting her have an orgasm. She should have known he wasn't going to let her off so easily.

Kaden climbed onto the bed, his back to the headboard. He lifted her onto his cock her knees going to the bed beside his hips. She was so wet she slid easily down his length. Her back arched in pleasure at the feel of him inside of her.

"Fuck me, Sawyer."

Her hips began moving, sliding his length deep inside her, finding a rhythm that drove her passion higher.

"Put your hands behind your back."

Sawyer's hands immediately crossed behind her back, which thrust her breasts out.

A moan slid past her lips when Kaden's hands glided to her pussy, spreading her pink flesh until she felt the flesh of his cock with every slide. His thumb rubbed her clit until the nub exploded into an orgasm that stopped her from moving.

A swat landed on her ass. "Did I tell you to stop?"

"No, Kaden." Sawyer rode out her climax on Kaden's cock, shuddering as he kept playing with her clit, not letting her body come down from her climax.

"Give me your tit."

Sawyer leaned forward until his mouth could reach her breast, keeping her hips moving.

Kaden's lips circled her breast, sucking her nipple into

his mouth where his tongue played with her nipple ring. Sawyer's body began to rebuild the fire while he continued stroking her breast into a hard nub before moving to the other one. Taking the breast in his mouth, his teeth grazed her nipple. Her stomach muscles rippled as another climax surged through her.

Kaden didn't let her stop. A bead of sweat slid between her breast, and his tongue licked the salty wetness.

Her thighs started to tremble from the strain of fucking him, and her pussy felt swollen from the number of climaxes around his cock. Tiny screams were now escaping as each climax led into another.

"I'm sorry, Kaden," Sawyer panted as his thumb continued to play with her clit. "I will never try to leave you again."

His teeth bit down on her nipple ring.

"I am so, so sorry. I won't even think about leaving you again, Kaden."

His cock thrust upwards as he suddenly rose up. Sawyer fell backwards on the mattress with Kaden's cock still buried deep inside of her. Her hands went to the mattress above her head, grabbing the sheets.

His hands went behind her knees, bringing her thighs high against her chest as he began to pound her with his thrusting cock.

"Why are you never going to leave me, Sawyer?"

His eyes blazed down into hers.

"Because you love me."

"Why are you never going to leave me, Sawyer?" he repeated.

"Because I love you."

Kaden's mouth found her, stifling his moan as his climax carried them both into a realm that only the two of them shared, each feeling what the other felt in their souls.

Kaden's body collapsed on her, his hands stroking her thighs until she managed to lower them back to the bed.

"Kaden, if that was meant as a punishment, I plan on

being bad, a lot," she said playfully.

Kaden laughed as he rolled to his side. "Woman, if you're going to challenge my authority, at least give me time to recover."

Sawyer giggled, jumping out of bed and going to the bathroom. Just before she shut the bathroom door, she bent down, wiggling her ass the way Vida had told her she would do at the end of every show.

Kaden lay staring at the closed bathroom door with his mouth open. A second later, he was manfully climbing out of the bed. He was never a man to pass up a challenge.

Chapter Twenty-seven

(Three Months Later)

Sawyer stepped out of the limo when the driver opened the door, waiting impatiently for Vida.

"Let's go; we're late."

"It's not my fault. You're the one who overslept." Sawyer blushed, remembering the late night she'd had with Kaden, which had resulted in her oversleeping. She opened the door to the office building that Kaden had rented a space in for the band's new tour manager.

"I haven't seen Jordan since Indiana. You're going to love her, Vida. Kaden rented this space for the next three months while she organizes the tour and straightens out R.J.'s mess. R.J.'s finances might be in a downward spiral with him in prison, but the band was smart enough to not give R.J. that type of control over their own assets.

"We can go out to lunch with her before hitting the furniture stores." Sawyer needed to buy more furniture to furnish the large house that Kaden had purchased not far from the one that Colton and Vida had purchased the previous month. Both women had decided to settle on the outskirts of Queen City. The city that they had once dreamed of escaping.

212

Vida had found her dream of living in a close-knit community, and Sawyer, sick of traveling, had enrolled in culinary school.

Sawyer and Vida strolled into Jordan's office, coming to a stop at the disorganized mess. Huge boxes were stacked in the middle of the floor. The office furniture had just been delivered and not yet placed. The small room looked like a tornado had been there.

Jordan's blonde head peeked over the filing cabinet.

"I know it looks terrible, but I'll have it in shape in no time." Her excited voice had both women smiling. You couldn't help liking the woman; her personality was so freaking bubbly. She reminded Sawyer of a bath bomb.

"I'm afraid I have to cancel lunch. I have another delivery coming, and I was hoping it would make it here before you arrived, but they just called. It's not going to happen. Can I take a rain check?"

"I can do better than that. Come by the house for dinner tonight. Vida and Colton can come. I'll even invite Brenley, Colton's sister. That way, you can get to know everyone at once."

"That sounds terrific." Jordan smiled, unwrapping a picture frame from bubble wrap and placing it on her desk before going to a box and taking out another one. Unwrapping it, she placed it on her desk as well. Vida helpfully moved the box closer to her desk.

Jordan took out another picture, unwrapping several layers of bubble wrap.

"Jordan, you really like bubble wrap, don't you?" Sawyer said jokingly.

"I learned my lesson. That bastard with Digger went through my suitcases. I just had these printed when he threw them all over the room."

"You must be close to your family," Sawyer said, picking up one of the frames from the desk.

Sawyer had a new respect for the woman who had a picture of a man whose appearance was dangerously lethal.

Vida whistled over her shoulder. No wonder Jordan hadn't been afraid of Max and Jackal; the man in the picture frame was staring back with a gravely serious expression. His blue gaze grabbed and held your attention, and that was just with a photograph.

"Jordan, if I wasn't head over heels in love with Kaden, I would beg for an introduction." Of course she would have to have a few drinks to work her courage up first.

"Sawyer, R.J. isn't around anymore and Kaden's already hired me. You can call me by my first name now." She laughed as Sawyer set the picture down and picked up another one, wanting to see another picture of the striking man.

"What is your first name?" she asked absently, only giving her half of her attention as she turned the picture frame toward her.

"Penni."

Sawyer stared down at the picture in her hand, almost fainting. Only Vida grabbing her for support had her able to hold on to her control.

Penni was in the picture, sitting on a huge boulder with green lush mountains behind her. Sitting next to her, laughing into the camera, was a beautiful, dark haired woman. She was dressed in a dress, and the girls were obviously trying to keep the wind from blowing it up. Her gentleness could easily be read in her face, just as the heart-wrenching sadness in her eyes couldn't be missed.

"W—who w—was the man in your picture?" Sawyer asked with a hoarse voice.

"That's my brother, Shade," Penni answered, staring at Sawyer curiously. "He looks kind of scary, but he can be sweet." Then she added, "Sometimes."

"Who's the woman?" Vida questioned with a tight voice.

"That was my college roommate, Lily. I already miss her. We became really close friends. She doesn't graduate until next semester." Penni took the picture frame from

Sawyer's hand, setting it carefully back down on the desk.

"I want to thank you, Sawyer, for convincing Kaden to give me that interview. I know he wouldn't have hired me without your help. I didn't make the best impression during my internship with R.J."

Sawyer didn't answer, gripping the desk for support. One of her nails broke, but she didn't feel the pain.

A knock sounded and Penni went to answer it. Sawyer and Vida gathered themselves during the reprieve. Seeing the deliverymen, they used the excuse to escape. Neither woman said a word until they were in the elevator. Vida was already crying when the elevator door closed.

"Oh, God. Oh, God. Oh, God!" Vida held on to the side of the elevator.

Sawyer weakly reached out, pressing the emergency stop on the elevator panel. Bursting into tears, she fell to her knees on the elevator floor.

"S—she's a—alive! She's alive!"

Vida came down next to her on the floor. Sawyer reached out, hugging her close as both of them cried.

"Callie's alive!"

Epilogue

Sawyer opened the door to the back porch, carefully balancing the two glasses of ice tea. She accidently spilt a few drops as she closed the door with her foot, remembering the days when she could hold two glasses in each hand. She didn't miss waitressing at all. She had enough people to wait on at home to fulfill that need.

Walking barefoot across the porch, she stepped carefully down the steps, determined not to spill any more. The grass felt wonderful on her feet as she walked across the yard.

"What took you so long?" Vida asked, taking her glass.

"I checked on Faith." Sawyer climbed on top of the picnic table beside Vida so that she could get a better look at the game going on across the yard. She took the baby monitor out of her pocket, laying it down next to her on the table.

"How much weight has she gained since her operation?"

"Three pounds," Sawyer said proudly. "The doctor said that was really good, that most babies born with drug addictions won't gain weight as fast," she said, relieved at the progress her adopted daughter was making.

"That's wonderful. Wait until she's old enough to eat your cooking; she will really start gaining weight."

"Mom!" A little boy haltingly ran across the yard, his crutches slowing him down.

"What?" Sawyer asked, seeing what the problem was before her son could answer.

"Roxi and Axel won't let me climb up the tree." Sawyer could understand their concern. His foot brace would make it almost impossible and they had been very protective of George since the adoption was final.

"Go tell your dad; he's strong enough to lift you up to the limb."

"Okay." Satisfied that his request would be granted, he turned around, searching for his father in the crowd. Her son was becoming a little spoiled. Sawyer leaned her face up to the sun, hiding her smile at Roxi and Axel's disgruntled looks.

"Colton hit a homerun." Vida stood up, jumping up and down on the bench.

Sawyer sat up, jerking her friend back down.

"Jeez, Vida. You trying to make them babies come early?"

"From your mouth to God's ear. I haven't seen my feet in a month."

"Enjoy it while you can. I don't envy you. Two crying babies at night. It was bad enough when George and Grace had ear infections and there was a year separating them in age. If Kaden hadn't been so much help and so good about getting up at night, I would have been terrified adopting them."

"I don't know why. You're a fantastic mom, Sawyer."

Sawyer grinned at her friend. She was blessed and she knew it as she watched George complain to his father.

Kaden picked up George, and with Colton's help, lifted him into the tree house with Grace. Roxi and Axel quickly climbed up the ladder, on the side of the tree, to play with their friends.

Both men started walking toward their wives.

"Did you ever think when we were little that we would get this lucky?"

"No. I didn't." Sawyer picked up her glass of tea, her tattoo catching her eye. The word freedom had several forget-me-nots wound through it, connecting it to a birdcage. Inside the birdcage, a tiny Robin sat on the perch, staring back with golden eyes. The cage was covered with flowers, and the vines spelling out Vida, Kaden and their children's names. The ink work was beautiful; Colton had done his best work on her. He had even scrolled Callie's name on the dangling cord, holding the key to the open cage door.

Also by Jamie Begley

The Last Riders Series:

Razer's Ride

Viper's Run

Knox's Stand

The VIP Room Series:

Teased

Tainted

Biker Bitches Series:

Sex Piston

The Dark Souls Series:

Soul Of A Man

About The Author

"I was born in a small town in Kentucky. My family began poor, but worked their way to owning a restaurant. My mother was one of the best cooks I have ever known, and she instilled in all her children the value of hard work, and education.

Taking after my mother, I've always love to cook, and became pretty good if I do say so myself. I love to experiment and my unfortunate family has suffered through many. They now have learned to steer clear of those dishes. I absolutely love the holidays and my family puts up with my zany decorations.

For now, my days are spent at work and I write during the nights and weekends. I have two children who both graduate this year from college. My daughter does my book covers, and my son just tries not to blush when someone asks him about my books.

Currently I am writing four series of books- The Last Riders, The Dark Souls, The VIP Room, and Biker Bitches series. My favorite book I have written is Soul Of A Woman, which I am hoping to release during the summer of 2014. It took me two years to write, during which I lost my mother, and brother. It's a book that I truly feel captures the true depths of love a woman can hold for a man. In case you haven't figured it out yet, I am an emotional writer who wants the readers to feel the emotion of the characters they are reading. Because of this, Teased is probably the hardest thing I have written.

All my books are written for one purpose- the enjoyment others find in them, and the expectations of my fans that inspire me to give it my best. In the near future I hope to take a weekend break and visit Vegas that will hopefully be this summer. Right now I am typing away on my next story and looking forward to traveling this summer!"

Jamie loves receiving emails from her fans,
JamieBegley@ymail.com

Find Jamie here,
https://www.facebook.com/AuthorJamieBegley

Get the latest scoop at Jamie's official website,
JamieBegley.net